Crossing the Line

Dianne (Di) Bates has written over 90 books for young readers including the prize-winning *The Last Refuge* which sold into Europe. Di has won national and state awards for her books, and has edited Australian children's magazines.

Currently she compiles *Buzz Words* (*The Latest Buzz on Children's Books*), an online magazine for people in the children's book industry.

Her website is:
www.enterprisingwords.com.

Also by Dianne Bates

CROSSING THE LINE

Dianne Bates

FORD ST

First published by Ford Street Publishing, an imprint of
Hybrid Publishers, PO Box 52, Ormond VIC 3204

Melbourne Victoria Australia

©2008

2 4 6 8 10 9 7 5 3 1

First published 2008

National Library of Australia Cataloguing-in-
Publication data:

Author: Bates, Dianne 1948-
Title: Crossing the Line / Dianne Bates

ISBN 9781876462703 (pbk.).

Target Audience: For children.

Subjects: Teenage girls – Juvenile fiction.
Depression in adolescence.
Self-mutilation.
Friendship in adolescence.
Women psychiatrists.
Therapist and patient.
Orphans.

Dewey Number: A823.3

Cover design © Grant Gittus Graphics
Text © Dianne Bates 2008
In-house editor: Saralinda Turner

Printed in Australia by McPherson's Printing Group

For my dearest husband, Bill Condon

1

A suitcase, my laptop computer and a backpack; this is what I bring with me. I've waited for this day for what seems like forever, counting down the hours, keeping my cool as much as I can. The house is a small bungalow no different from other redbrick houses in the suburb, a short walking distance to the railway station and the shops.

Marie briskly rings the front doorbell then steps back, surveying the uncut front lawn and tongue-clicking at the avalanche of garbage erupting from a split plastic bag on the porch.

'Yep?' The door is opened by a tall skinny girl with a face full of metal and a towel wrapped around her, her molasses-coloured hair stringy and damp from the shower.

'I understand you were expecting us. The room for rent? I believe it's all been arranged. Someone from the Department would have spoken to you.' Marie pulls out a business card. Her manner, as usual, is prickly.

The girl rolls her eyes. 'We knew you were coming.

Didn't think you'd want a frigging red carpet.' My heart thumps with applause. Anyone who can tick Marie off as obviously as she's ticked at the moment is an instant buddy.

Suddenly there's a guy behind the girl. He's dressed in jeans and a T-shirt. And he's cute, grinning with the whitest set of teeth you'd see on any TV commercial. 'Come on in,' he says.

His hand brushes against mine as he takes my bags. 'Here, let me.' Our eyes meet. His are green, flecked with little dots of translucent colours, gemstones of amber and opal. Very nice.

In the living room Marie's disapproval is palpable as she stares openly and rudely around her, noting, I'm sure, the furniture covered in junk, the slight odour of cat poo, even the carpet fluff and wine stains.

Cute boy shoves a jumble of clothes onto the floor to clear a chair. Then he pushes aside magazines from the sofa. 'Sorry about that.' Again with the brilliant smile.

The girl has disappeared.

'I'm Sophie,' I say. 'I love your place.'

'Matt.' He shakes my hand, looks directly into my eyes again. He's so gorgeous! 'I hope you like it here with Amy and me.'

Mrs Rules and Regulations takes over then. I've heard it all before and can't wait for her to buzz off. Thank god she doesn't stick around for long.

The moment she's gone, Amy appears. 'What a bitch! Is she your case worker?'

I nod, and suddenly it's as though someone has pumped laughing gas into the room. The three of us crack up. Oh, I'm so happy! This is what I've wanted for so long; my first taste of Freedom.

Amy and Matt don't waste any time in making me feel at home. With Marie gone, they take me on a house inspection. Like the living room, the rest of the place is messy, but it's a nice sort of messy, not filthy, just lived-in. Amy's proud of the backyard which is mostly overgrown but she's been digging out a section in the sun for a herb and veggie garden. 'I haven't been living here long.' She gazes around her. 'It'll take a while. Maybe you'd like to help?'

'Sure,' I say. 'Why not?'

'We're going to make dinner for you,' Matt says when I've checked out everything. He grins and I try hard not to drool. 'Take your time and come out when you're ready.'

They leave me alone while I unpack my stuff. Mine is the smallest of the three bedrooms, but I don't mind. Not only is it my own, but it even has a latch inside the door which means I won't have anyone barging in whenever they feel like it as I've had in the past with foster parents and their kids. This is where I've wanted to be ever since I can remember, away from the watchful eye of strangers: my own space.

I'll still be under Marie's care and with two flatmates, but at least they are close to my age and both seem really cool.

Someone knocks on my door. It's Matt, waiting for me to open it, not assuming it's okay to come in without my say so. I'm impressed.

'Dinner!' he announces.

I've had better meals than their chickpea curry and rocket salad, but this is the first time in ages that I've shared food with company I like.

'I prefer a thick, bloody steak,' Matt says, 'but Amy's a vegetarian and . . .'

'. . . what Amy says goes,' butts in Amy. She looks so determined and bossy that Matt and I laugh.

'In your dreams,' Matt tells her.

After the meal we settle down in the living room, Matt with a beer, me with a red wine opened specially for the occasion, and Amy sucking on a joint. She offers both of us a puff, but we decline. I tried smoking marijuana once but it made me feel light-headed then sleepy.

'So, tell us about yourself,' Amy says without preamble.

I tell as much as I want, how I was raised by an aunt and uncle until I was about eleven and then they broke up, and how I was fostered for the first time.

I find out that Amy and Matt have both had

4

dealings with the Department. Amy's been through the foster system, same as me, but Matt isn't willing to go into his story. 'It's complicated,' is all he'll say.

'I was twelve when I was first fostered,' Amy says. 'It was really hard getting used to living with another family. And then there was another family. And another.'

We nod at one another. Been there, done that.

'I've lost count of how many foster carers I've had,' I tell them. 'About six weeks ago my last fostering broke down. The Department put me in a youth refuge but I spat the dummy. It was such a dump. Told Marie I was seventeen, that I'd leave school and get a job and there was nothing she or the Department could do about it. But it didn't work out. I stuffed up . . .'

Amy, her cat Persia on her lap, pauses from smoking. Matt puts down his beer.

Oh no, I've said too much. Opened my big mouth. Regular habit.

'Don't stop there,' says Amy.

'What did you do?' Matt asks.

I am definitely not going to tell them details about the overdose. None of their business. Instead, I lie.

'Nothing major. Boring stuff. But you know how the Department is – they overreacted. I had to go to a case management conference . . .'

'Hate them,' Amy interjects. 'If you sneeze they want it in triplicate.'

'. . . and it was suggested that if I *behaved* myself and stayed on at school, they might find a new place for me to live while I finished my last year. A good place, for once.'

Amy nods. 'Right. So then I get a phone call from this guy I know at the Department who thinks it would be a good idea if . . .'

'You moved in with us,' Matt concludes.

'Yeah, and I grabbed it with both hands.' I smile. 'This is a whole new beginning for me. New place to live. And I start at my new school tomorrow.'

Amy sighs heavily.

'Sometimes I wish I was still at school.' She sits on the carpet, her back against a chair. 'I hated it when I was there but maybe I should have tried a bit harder. Still, I guess you don't need an education to be a tattoo artist.'

'Is that what you do?' I say.

'Hope to. One day. It's hard to find someone who'll give me a start.'

'You'll get there.' I squeeze her shoulder. 'Don't give up.'

'You at school, Matt?' I ask.

He shakes his head. 'Nah. TAFE. Part-time. Still have a couple of years to go.'

There's a short pause. I feel that I've said enough about my life. For now. Time to change the subject. 'So, how does this place run?'

Amy takes the lead. 'We buy our own groceries

and share the rent, electricity and phone bills.'

'Well, in theory we share the phone bills,' Matt adds.

'You on about the phone again?' Amy counters.

'Who, me? Just because you still owe the kitty ten bucks?'

'Hey, I paid that. Then I took it out again to pay myself for cleaning the toilet because you didn't do it.'

'I missed one time!'

'Okay, but then I fined you for leaving the seat up.'

'I'll leave the seat up whenever I like.'

'Time out, you guys!' I interject, but the argument continues.

'Not in my house, you won't!'

'But this isn't your house!'

I put my fingers in my mouth and whistle as hard as I can.

It stops them cold. They both stare at me.

'I can fix this,' I say. 'Let's take a vote. All those in favour of the toilet seat being left up, raise your hand.'

Matt's hand is the only one to go up.

'Those against . . .'

'Ha-ha,' smirks Amy as she and I raise our hands.

'Sorry, Matt,' I say. 'You lose. Bad luck.'

'I demand a re-count,' he says. But he's grinning.

Amy smiles at me. 'I reckon you'll fit in just fine

here, Sophie. Two girls against one loser guy: now he hasn't got a chance.'

That night. Sleeping. I am sketching in my dreams a scene of my childhood. Perspective doesn't matter; everything is distorted and oblique as it is when you're very young. My Aunt Arlene and Uncle Dutch's faces loom large and clearly defined. Next, they are diminished and pale, like ghosts wafting in and out of sight. Sometimes they float close by and reach out and touch me. I am tucked between crisp white sheets that smell faintly of lavender, and Arlene is leaning over me, her ginger-ale hair lapping against my cheek, her face a mask, eyes hooded, skin mottled in shadow. She whispers to me in her sing-song voice, a children's rhyme from the Netherlands. Dutch is beside her, huge and gentle like the Big Friendly Giant in that wonderful book he used to read to me before bedtime. And then, just as suddenly as they came to me, they are gone, and I'm alone, stretching out my hand and crying, begging them to come back, to take me with them.

2

'Lost?'

Her hair is dyed bright red and blue and sticks out from her head in dozens of braids. She has a nose ring and ear studs.

I'm standing at the school entrance trying to work out where the admin office is, while dozens of kids mill around me, shouting, swearing, talking on mobile phones, punching one another. It's a jungle, and now there's this odd-looking girl grinning at me.

'Hi.' Her smile reveals teeth white and perfectly formed. 'You're new around here.'

I'm always the new girl.

'I guess so.'

'You got a name?'

'Sophie.'

'I'm Greta Murphy. Doing your final year?'

I nod.

'Good luck. Teachers treat you like slaves here. But most of them are okay. Except for Jenkins. He's the deputy principal. We call him Mud Guards: all shiny on the top but dirty as hell underneath. You don't want to get on his bad side.'

She talks at a hundred kays per hour, almost without drawing breath.

'Come on, I'll take you to the office.' She grabs my arm and proceeds to charge through the throng.

'Outta my way, coming through!' she yells. The crowd parts. As we move along, she's greeted from all sides. A popular girl.

'What school were you at before here?' she shouts above the playground noise.

'Cheltenham.'

Greta halts abruptly. I almost collide with her.

'That private college? The one that charges thousands in fees?' Her face is close-up and personal; her eyes are unsettling – blue as summer sky and burning into me.

Almost ashamed to admit it, I nod.

'Ohmigod! Your parents must be loaded.'

It's too complicated to explain about my 'family', not that I'd want to anyway, especially to a stranger in the middle of a crowd, so I just shrug.

'Why'd you leave?'

How nosy is this Greta? I say the first thing that springs into my mind.

'Expelled.'

She grins. 'I like you already. I expect all the juicy details at recess. Don't leave out a word.'

We're now at the office counter.

Greta gives me a thumbs-up. 'You should be okay now. I'll catch you later.'

'Okay.'

'Give 'em hell!' She smiles all the way to China and gallops off as a bell rings.

I wait. I seem to spend half my life waiting. Waiting in Department office rooms mainly, but also in new school reception areas. I figure with all of my fosters since Arlene and Dutch I've been to seven schools. There's always paperwork: name, address, former address and so on. God, I wish they'd hurry up.

'Sophie?'

It's the office assistant.

'Mr Jenkins is ready to see you.'

I enter the office. He's sitting at his desk, eyes down, writing. He doesn't look up for the next five minutes. Arrogant pig. What is it about some men in power? He knows I'm here. Is it too much for him to show me just the tiniest bit of respect? Yes, way too much, obviously.

Offices tell a lot about people. His is as tidy as. Everything at ninety degree angles. There's a shelf full of books, every one of them in alphabetical order. He's anally retentive, that's for sure.

Finally his face. Smiling. Big phoney.

'Sophie!' He says my name like an emcee announcing a stripper. Sleazebag.

'Welcome to Cromer High.'

He pauses. Susses me out.

I maintain a blank face.

'I see from your paperwork . . .' Head down again, he flips through the thick sheaf of my school records. 'You've been to quite a few schools . . .' Head bobs up. 'It looks like you've had a few problems here and there.' Smile like a barracuda.

'Just a few.' I do my Nice Girl act. It won't hurt to get on his good side – if he's got one.

'Yes. Hmm. Despite this you've maintained a very high grade average.' Another barracuda job. 'We like smart students at Cromer.'

He sure is smooth, trying to appeal to my ego – and succeeding. Yes, I do well at school, and yes, they've said I'm bright. I really love the challenge of learning and so far getting good grades has been the one constant in my life.

'Now, young lass, let's go through a few things.'

I bridle at his condescending tone, but keep it together.

'Yes, sir.'

We discuss my workload and the looming final exams. I want to go on to uni next year so I need high marks. Not that I'm quite sure what I plan to do with the rest of my life. I love writing, especially poetry, so journalism sounds like a good option. Though journalists don't write poetry, do they? It's all so confusing sometimes. School. Jobs. Life. I wonder how anyone gets through it.

My mind is drifting as Jenkins blabs on until

he stands and says, 'Right. Time to meet your classmates.'

It's always this way: a blur of faces, every one of them checking out the new girl. And a welcoming teacher who has no idea who I am. I keep a stone face and sit where I'm told, staring ahead at the blackboard. I don't make friends easily; in fact long ago I gave up trying to be liked. I'm always moving on pretty quickly – hello, goodbye. So why bother in the first place?

'Hey, Sophie!'

It's Greta. I hadn't noticed her sitting a few seats away. Her face lights up and she winks. I wonder why she's so friendly. Probably gay. Just my luck.

At lunchtime she latches on to me. 'You've gotta meet my friends!'

This is different. During break times I've always lurked around alone, totally ignored. I'm not exactly shy, but charging straight up to complete strangers and expecting them to cheerfully include me in their group is just not my style. Greta's a true original, doesn't seem to give a stuff what others think of her. She insists that I sit with her and her friends in a grassy corner of the schoolyard.

'Tell us,' Greta says, 'we're all dying to hear – how did you get expelled from Cheltenham?'

My little white lie has snowballed into something huge. If I can keep it going I might end up a legend. But do I want to lie to Greta and these guys? No, not really.

As I'm working out what to say, a gangly Year 10 boy barges up and shouts, 'Hey, Greta, I hear Brian Pausacker's got the hots for you!'

'That loser!'

My new friends all hoot with laughter, Greta the loudest. 'Tell him I've already got a boyfriend, and even if I didn't, I'd rather suck on a lemon than go anywhere near that gross face of his!'

So perhaps she's not gay at all – maybe she just likes me . . .

The other girls also give the boy heaps, and he racks off as fast as his skinny legs will let him. Maya, who sits to my left, is the quietest and the most conservative of the group – the opposite of Greta. No studs or rings, no off-the-wall hairstyle. She shares her sandwiches with me because, in my anxiety about the new school, I forgot to pack lunch or bring any money. The others are friendly, too. One offers to give me a spare textbook, while another promises to photocopy English literature notes so I'll be up to speed. I feel completely at ease with them all and can't believe my good luck. At the same time, a small voice is nagging at the back of my mind, telling me not to get too involved. So many times I've been in relationships that break down. It's hard to trust. Still, what matters is the moment, and the moment, for now, is good.

3

*W*hile the rest of the world is asleep, I hop onto Matt's bike – which he said to borrow anytime – and head off. I love this time of the day before people intrude with their busyness and the air is fresh. The streets are deserted as I cycle through suburbia until I come to the pool: beaches on both sides of it stretching golden and unbroken to the next headlands.

I have the water all to myself. In I step, cautiously, gasping and heart thudding, toes, ankle, shins, thighs, ever deeper. Head under . . . Oh! It's freezing!

And then I launch into the first lap, gliding away from the world. As I swim, light flickers to create washes of watercolour swirling in arcs of cellophane greens and silvers. The world below my goggled face is a repetition of concrete and lichen. As I follow a crack that runs the length of the pool my body ceases to exist. Vaguely I'm aware that behind me the water churns as I glide forward, arms rotating, over and through, over and through, on and on.

Now there is nothing within me but peace.

When my body tires and I'm almost out of breath,

I become aware of others moving around the pool, on the blocks, beside me in the water. That's when the magic ends.

Amy's at the breakfast table, head poised over the Saturday newspaper, circling ads in the classifieds.

'Not looking for a new place, I hope?' I squat beside her with a bowl of muesli.

'No.' She looks up. 'Garage sales. I love them. Ever been to one?'

'Nope.'

'Matt makes fun of me, but half the stuff in our place I bought way cheap at sales.'

She points out a couple of chairs, the curtains, a stack of CDs, a print on the wall.

'I'm just about to go. Wanna come?'

Before long we're in Amy's VW bug, roaring down streets. She speeds like she's out to win a Grand Prix, takes corners on two wheels, swears and honks at other drivers.

'This your car?' I ask, wondering how she can afford one on the youth allowance.

'A friend's,' she says.

Curious, I dig deeper. 'How old are you, Amy?'

'Old enough.'

'Yeah, sure. But are you old enough to have a licence?'

'You know what?' she says. 'There's too much red tape in this world. Why do I need a licence? I can

16

drive. Look at me. I'm doing fine, aren't I?'

Suddenly she swerves to avoid a pedestrian, just missing him.

'See?' She grins. 'Only a top driver could have got out of that.'

At the first stop we check out tables chocka with all sorts of junk. Nothing much interests me, but Amy's stockpiling – glassware, cutlery, a crimson scarf, an astrology book (no back cover), cute ornaments . . .

'Look at this!' she keeps exclaiming. .

When it comes to buying, she's a mistress of the barter.

'Fifteen dollars.'

'Are you kidding me?'

'All right – ten. But I won't go any lower.'

'That's a rip-off – see you later.'

'Wait.' Deep sigh. 'What's your offer?'

Finally she gives the poor man five dollars and she's the proud owner of a boxful of assorted junk – though she calls it treasure.

Then we're on to the next sale.

It's funny how people sell their belongings for a song. I don't have much, but what I do have is for keeps. My things are part of who I am. What I treasure most is the stuff from my life with Arlene and Dutch. Photos mostly, but toys and books, too. I've kept a nightgown with tiny pink and purple el-ephants on it that Arlene used to wear. Sometimes when I'm lonely and missing them, I hunker down under my doona and hold the nightie close to my face. I imagine Arlene's smell and the feel of her arms around me. Dopey, I know, but still, that's what I do.

'You having fun, Sophie?' Amy grinds the car gears and curses again at a driver who's too slow. I grin, and nod.

All up we visit ten sales. After about five I'm over it. Not Amy. 'I do this every Saturday morning,' she tells me proudly. 'Love it!'

After the sales we park at the local mall and wander from shop to shop, mostly checking out new CDs. Amy's into New Age music. I like it too, and she promises to record her favourite chill-out tracks for me. I think of her full-on driving and decide she needs to have some calming music on in the VW – playing loudly.

'Must get some incense!' She makes it sound like it's life or death. I tag along as she charges into a store. Several minutes later, after much deliberation, I hear: 'Should I get musk or vanilla?'

I presume this is a question for me. But she answers it herself.

'What the hell, I'll get them both.'

Then, before I realise what she's up to, she's stuck two boxes into her skirt waistband and is ambling down the aisle looking like innocence personified.

'Move it,' she says. 'We're outta here.' She strolls

ahead and I pretend not to be with her. I can't believe she's so brazen about shoplifting.

'You could have been caught!' I say when we're away from the store.

'No chance.' She smiles at me like she should be congratulated. 'They never miss it. Besides they overcharge like crazy. Incense is much cheaper at the markets.'

I'm thinking: So why don't you buy it there – instead of stealing? But I keep it inside my head. I don't want to get offside with her when I've just moved in. It's easier to let it go. Still, I don't like it.

'It's just a bit of fun,' Amy says. And then, as though reading my mind, she adds, 'Don't worry, I never nick stuff from friends.'

We're having a chai tea later at home when our conversation turns to Matt. Actually, I've steered it in his direction.

'So how available is he?'

Amy raises her eyebrows. 'You interested?'

'Not particularly.'

'Me either. Anyway, I don't know him much more than you.'

'How come? You share a place with him.'

'Yeah, but only for a few weeks. I'm almost as new as you, Sophie – or is Soph better? Which one do you like?'

I'm about to say I'll take anything, but then a

dash of Amy's mad personality rubs off on me and I tell her grandly, 'You may call me Sophia . . . Lady Sophia.'

'I'll call you a goose!' she replies, as we both laugh.

'Sophie, Soph – both are fine,' I say.

'Anyway,' she pauses to take a sip of her tea. 'About Matt – all I can tell you is that there's a photo of him and a girl in his room. She's got her arms around him so maybe she's his girlfriend.'

I thank her for that info but can't help wondering what she was doing in his room. I've had enough snooping in my life. Hate it. I do like Amy but I don't know yet if I trust her. I tell myself, *be careful*.

'Come here, My Lady.' Amy beckons me over. 'I'm going to braid your hair.' I go along with it. Keeps her happy. And secretly, I like the closeness of it. She spends the next two hours, when she could be doing a dozen other things, attending to and transforming me.

'You look gorgeous.' She angles the mirror on all sides so I can check out what she's done.

'Not true . . . But thanks, Amy. Thank you.'

A strange chick, this Amy. Generous. Impulsive. Shoplifter. Snoop. But friend, too, I hope.

Later that afternoon I duck down to the shops and buy a posy of roses as a thank you for her kindness.

4

I love my new place. True, it's often messy, but it's my first real home since Arlene and Dutch. Living with Amy and Matt is great. We're equals.

Today Matt invites Amy and me to a soccer match.

'It's our team's grand final,' he explains.

'So why should that interest me?' asks Amy.

'I'm playing.' Matt glares. 'It's us Rebels versus the Eagles, didn't you know?'

Amy snorts into her coffee. 'So you're inviting us to sit in rain, hail and snow and watch you he-men run around for hours and hours playing with a ball, and we're supposed to cheer our guts out?'

Matt's face colours. 'Well, if you're not up to it . . . '

'I'd love to go,' I volunteer, sneaking a sideways look at Amy. I'm as keen about soccer as she is – watching grass grow is more entertaining but I figure some time alone with Matt is worth a little sacrifice. She shakes her head and casts her eyes upward as if I've put the feminist cause back a few hundred years.

'Have fun. I'm going away for the weekend anyway.' Amy shrugs. 'Not that I'd go if I were here.

pid game.'

Matt returns fire. 'Yeah, I suppose it is boring – if you're too dumb to understand the rules.'

'What's to understand? You kick the ball and if you can't get to it you punch whoever's closest. Isn't that how it works?'

'Wow.' Matt grins. 'You sound just like my coach.'

'Hey.' Amy points a finger at him. 'If I were your coach I'd tell you to try holding your breath – for an hour or so.'

Matt pauses to think of a snappy reply. But Amy blocks her ears.

'For once,' she says, 'I'm having the last word.'

He nods, admitting defeat.

'I'll be in my room when you're ready, Matt,' I say, trying to look eager, but of course not too eager.

'Sucked in,' Amy mutters.

With time to puddle around, I gaze out through the window onto the busy street. At last the Department has given me an allowance to buy some curtains. Now I wonder what colour and pattern to choose. Something soft and pretty. Yeah. There's money in the budget too for bed linen and a new doona . . . I could make this room really special.

As I move about, pulling up my bedcovers and picking up clothes, I make a mental note of what I need: a bedside lamp, maybe some posters. Desiderata, which I love. Or a photo of a beach on a sunny day. So this is what 'home' feels like . . .

Snuggled up on the bed, I think about writing a poem in my journal. Out the window I watch leaves swishing around on a tree. For so long I was like those leaves, blown about and bossed. Finally I have some control of my life.

All too soon Matt taps on the door. 'You ready?'

'Sure am.'

I grab my jacket, hide my journal, and we're off.

'Thanks for coming, Soph.'

He opens the door of his van for me. I act as though I'm accustomed to this gallantry.

'I don't mind,' I say. 'Good day for a drive.'

'Perfect.' He turns on his bright smile. And the day looks even better.

There are only the two front seats in the van. The back is crammed with boxes and masses of tools. Matt notices me giving it the once over, and I get the naughty schoolboy grin.

'Sorry about the mess.' He shrugs. 'What can I do? It just keeps following me around . . . I'll clean it up one of these days . . . Maybe.'

I'd like to ask him what's in the boxes, but he might be a mad bomber and that knowledge would very likely ruin the day, so I don't ask. But as the engine roars to life, he volunteers the answer anyway. 'Got all my workshop gear in there. I'm into making things.'

'Yeah, like what?' I'm glad to have something to talk about.

'I'm doing this course at college . . .'

Little by little he joins the dots that make up his life. Nothing personal yet, but I'm patient. His face glows when he tells me about an award he won at high school.

'It was a national science competition – you know, hundreds of kids would have entered. Got lucky there. Bit of bribery never hurts!'

His face has road maps when he laughs. When he gets really old there'll be deep grooves in it. But I like that kind of face.

'You didn't bribe anyone,' I say. 'What did you win it for?'

'Aw, just some fruit-picking gadget. No one ever manufactured it – all too hard and expensive. But winning the prize was good. Made me think about being an inventor. That's why I took this course in engineering.'

Not once, as we drive, are there any awkward gaps in our conversation. Matt opens up like he doesn't when Amy's around.

At last, I think, a guy with some brains. And ambition. The boys at my new school – and they are all boys, not mature like Matt – generally seem so childish that I wouldn't want to hang with them. Matt talks about all sorts of things, the neighbourhood, our house – and, most impressive of all – he even asks questions about me. With some guys, I really don't think they realise there are other people in the universe. Matt wants to know about my hobbies, subjects I like at school. He sidesteps any delicate areas, which I appreciate. One day we might get to talk about the tricky bits of both our lives. Too soon yet. Now it's just good to talk, nice and easy.

I ask him about Amy, sure there has to be a problem. Seems to me they're always fighting.

He sees it differently. 'Nah, it's not fighting. We bump heads now and then, that's all. We're good mates, really. It's just that Amy wants to be the boss of the world and she can't, because that's my job.' He chuckles to himself, and then adds, 'I wish.'

Matt switches off the engine, reaches over for his sports bag and then turns to me. 'Well, here we are! Hope you like the game.'

'Sure I will,' I say. 'Soccer's great.'

Did I really say that? Oh boy, I'm glad Amy didn't hear me.

'Trust me,' he says, 'it's going to be fun.'

I follow him over to the clubhouse where there's a cluster of supporters and guys dressed in Matt's blue and white colours. I get the usual round of introductions and handshakes – too many names to remember.

'She's my flatmate,' Matt insists when someone ribs him about me being his new girl. I nod, backing him up, but I'm quietly pleased that anyone would think that.

'See ya soon.' Matt winks as he and his team troop

25

onto the field, while I'm left alone with the soccer groupie crowd. Most of them are girls my age or slightly older, probably here to cheer on their boyfriends. One of them notices that I look a bit lost so she comes over.

'I'm Tracey,' she tells me. 'My guy's out there doing his thing. We're getting married. Boyd. Did you meet him? Spiky red hair. Tall.' She points him out.

'Aw, yeah. I see him.'

She moves closer. 'Now just between us – what's this I hear about you and Matt? Are you two seeing each other?'

I shake my head. 'No, nothing like that. I'm just his flatmate. There's another girl who lives with us, too. Amy.'

'Oh. Right.'

'And she's not his girlfriend either,' I add.

'Well. Fascinating.'

'What's so fascinating, Tracey?'

'You're the first girl he's ever brought to a game.'

I shrug. *Disinterested. Don't care. So what?*

I hope she buys it.

Of course I care. It's intriguing, promising. It makes me happy. But then I rein myself in – *slow down, Sophie* – I'm in no hurry for the whole boyfriend-girlfriend thing. I'm too tied up with my final year schoolwork for that. Don't need the hassle. Nah. Forget it . . . well, for a while anyway.

We watch as Matt passes the ball to Boyd. He

pokes around, feints to the left; lofts it to Matt who lets it bounce off his chest. He's not too shabby and neither is Boydie boy. Together they weave in and out of opponents, passing the ball to one another until they're in sight of the goal posts.

'Go, Boyd!' screams Tracey.

'Come on, Matt!' I squeal. It really is exciting. Much more so than I expected.

Matt rights himself, and then goes for it. The ball pings off his boot and thumps into the back of the net. We all explode with an almighty, 'Yeah!' Hugs and backslaps all around.

'Our boys are the best,' Tracey roars above the din.

'Go the Eagles!' someone shouts close by.

I just have to reply to that. 'Go the Rebels!'

At half-time Matt's beaming face is spattered with muck. 'That goal was for you!' He gives me a high five and a smile that I know I'll keep.

Before long the second half is on. It's kind of exciting except I have a distinct feeling of deja vu. Pass, kick, head butt, jump and scream. Yes, that seems familiar. Finally, the full-time whistle is blown without another goal being scored. Why did they bother?

'What did you think?' asks Matt when he comes off the field.

'It was brilliant,' I lie.

Everyone gathers in the clubhouse for lunch and drinks. I don't see much of Matt – he and his team are huddled together doing the boy-talk thing. Eventually he comes over with Boyd, who turns out to be his best buddy. Tracey's there, too.

Boyd does the talking. 'Short notice I know, Sophie, but how'd you like to come to a barbecue at our place this arvo? With Matt, of course. He's already invited.'

'It's our little girl Charlotte's first birthday,' Tracey adds.

'Sure, I'd love to.' I turn to Matt. 'If it's okay with you. I don't want to butt in or anything.'

'Hey.' Matt grips my shoulder. 'Of course it's okay with me. It was my idea to ask you.'

'Okay.' Somehow I manage to say it casually. That's really hard to do when I'm floating.

At Tracey's place Matt deserts me. The minute we walk through the front door, he's away with the guys like I don't exist. Typical male. They head straight to the backyard and start milling around the barbecue, drinking beer and carrying on like burning a few snags is some major life achievement. He's officially demoted from the pedestal I'd put him on. I'm alone and feeling awkward, wishing I was someplace else.

'Did he go off and leave you, Sophie?' It's Tracey, an apron wrapped around her waist. 'Come into the kitchen, I need a hand.' She guides me through the living room which is filled with people of all ages, most of them older – twenties and thirties, lounging around gossiping. Toddlers are climbing over their legs and a bunch of kids run around, chasing one another and squealing. Someone's strung up balloons and a *Happy Birthday* sign.

'Know how to make a garden salad?' Tracey shoves a lettuce and tomatoes at me. 'This is my mum,' she adds. 'Hesba, meet Sophie.'

Hesba's up to her elbows in potato salad. She's about the same age as Arlene but bottle-blonde with dark roots. She smiles at me. 'Hello, love, welcome to our crazy household.'

Near the sink, there's a chubby little girl in a high chair, her hands gooey-full of cake. She's got bright green eyes, masses of golden curls and the sweetest face which is smeared all over with half-eaten muck.

'This is Charlotte.' Tracey swipes a washer over the baby's face. 'Little greedy-guts, aren't you, my precious bubby?'

'She's lovely,' I tell her. And she is.

'You got any brothers or sisters, love?' Hesba dodges past me to get to the fridge.

'No, but I really love little kids.' Then, remembering some of my fosters' kids, I add, 'Well, most of the time I love them.'

'I know exactly what you mean.' She points at Tracey. 'Ratbag of a baby, this one.'

'Mum!'

'You were. Painting on the walls, throwing tantrums.'

'Okay, okay. But that was then. I'm really good now, aren't I?'

'No. You're exactly the same.'

29

'Mum! I am not!'

It's all good-natured banter. Just a mum and daughter having fun. I feel relaxed and comfortable around them. The feeling continues later, when I run the introduction gauntlet.

'This is Sophie,' Tracey says. 'Matt's new flatmate.'

Great. No pressure. There are a few winks and nudges from some old codger who thinks he's funny, when he's really only pathetic.

'Every family's got one,' Hesba says when Uncle Herbie toddles off. 'Don't mind him.'

I hope he gets run over by a passing rhino.

Out in the backyard we arrange the salads and other savouries on a long trestle table, while Boyd and Matt fork sausages and steaks onto a stream of plates. I've attended lots of parties like this where I've not known anyone except my fosters, but today seems different. Even though I'm here for the first time, it's sort of like I belong. Tracey's been a big part of that.

Working with her back in the kitchen, brewing coffee and dunking teabags, she tells me a little about Matt. I'm interested in all of it, but one part in particular, jolts me.

'His parents and older sister, Jenny, were killed in a car accident.'

'That's awful.'

'Yeah. He took it hard. Went off the rails a bit.

You know, mixed in with a bad crowd, used to get into fights – he had a temper back then – oh my, did he ever.'

'I had no idea.'

'Yes, but anyway, that's all in the past. He sorted himself out and now he's a great guy. Just like part of our family. He's even Charlotte's godfather.'

I glance at Matt through the window. He's probably reliving every minute of the big game with his mates. He looks up and sees me, waves and smiles. I wish he was in here with me, but I don't mind so much now. I want him to be happy.

'And now that you're part of his life,' Tracey adds, 'you're welcome here any time, Sophie.'

There really aren't words for how that makes me feel. I thank her with a smile, and hope she knows how much I mean it.

On the drive home, Matt quietly says, 'They liked you.'

I'm not sure how to respond.

'The way you were with little Charlotte, it was great to see.'

I rub at a stain the baby's left on my top. Chocolate ice-cream. 'I'm used to looking after kids. They're easy. I want to have at least four of my own.'

Matt grins. 'Only four? There's eleven in a soccer team.'

'Really? Well, sorry, pal, but I don't like soccer quite that much.'

We both laugh. It's good, it's all so good. But then suddenly the conversation dries up. Silence builds and builds until I have to say something – anything.

'Tracey told me about your family. I'm really sorry. Was it long ago?'

Matt glares at me. It's a look I haven't seen before. Bad choice of conversation.

'Oops . . . sorry. You don't have to answer.'

There's still more silence before he finally speaks.

'I don't like talking about that stuff.' He looks straight ahead at the road.

'Sure, sure, that's fine,' I splutter. 'I understand. I had no business mentioning it.'

'Maybe some other time.'

'All right, but only if you want to. Anytime you want to talk about it, I'm here.'

Matt checks the rear-vision mirror before making a right-hand turn. 'You've got a deal,' he says.

A few days later Matt comes home early and we find ourselves with a rare moment alone. We move around one another in the kitchen making hot drinks. Both of us raid the fridge and wander into the living room to put our feet up.

'I'm totally stuffed.' He drops his head dramatically to his chest. 'It's so good to relax.'

'Tough day at college?'

'More than that. I've taken on extra work at the growers' market.' He chomps into his sandwich.

'Need the money. And man, is it hard going.'

His defences are down. Guess he's too tired to care. He talks freely about his job, the guys he works with, the trip he's going to take when, and if, he saves enough money. He wants to go to South America, see a toucan in the wild.

'Might only be a dream,' he says, shaking his head and grinning. 'Probably won't ever get there – but hey, you gotta have dreams, right?'

'Right, Matt. Definitely.'

We talk some more about ordinary things. Then he stops and looks at me. He doesn't say a word but I know what's on his mind. I nod, trying to let him know that it's okay, that I'm here for him. That he can trust me.

'It was almost two years ago,' he says, his fingers playing arpeggio on the couch arm. 'I didn't have any other rellos and I'd just turned sixteen, so the Department tried to run my life for a while. That lasted about five minutes before I got jack of it. I found ways of getting by on my own.'

I don't come straight out and ask him what ways he's talking about, but he sees the question in my eyes, and answers it.

'You know, bank robbery, kidnapping – stuff like that.'

'Idiot.' I hit him with a cushion, but I'm grateful that he's cut through the tension. And so glad he has a sense of humour.

'The stupid thing is,' Matt continues, 'I keep feeling guilty about the accident. I should have been killed too.'

I don't say anything because I'm sure he's heard it all before. Sometimes listening is the best you can do.

'People tell me it's only natural to feel that way. It takes a long time to get over it, blah, blah. It's all true, but it doesn't make it any easier.'

I'd like to hug him, tell him he's not alone, but I just don't know him well enough.

'It's going to be okay,' I say.

'You bet it is.' He's got his brave face back on.

A few days later when the Department deposits my allowance into my bank account, I spend ages window-shopping, looking for something special for Matt. I find a fantastic book about inventions, and when I give it to him, his jaw drops.

'For me?'

'Yep.'

'For why?'

'For sharing,' I say.

He nods, and I know he understands.

5

*N*oel Palmer's my shrink. It's his job to let me talk about whatever I want, or so he explained during our first session. He's a short, dark-haired man with olive skin and brown eyes that look inflamed around the edges. He often sneezes so I think he suffers from hay fever. Or maybe he's allergic to something. Probably nut cases like me! Typically, he perches on the edge of his chair, fingers intertwined and face intent, listening to me as if everything I say ought to be awarded a trophy.

I've been coming here since my last fostering broke down. Don't know any more about him than I did that first day I walked into his office. He could be a serial killer for all I know – a cat burglar, rapist, man with a wicked past, wanted on six continents! Most likely he has a boring life – married with two-point-one children, sex on Saturday, church on Sunday, listening to people's confessions the rest of the week.

Call me dumb as, but I'm still not really sure what Noel wants me to say during this therapy business. If I ask him a question, like, 'What do you want me to talk about?' he invariably asks me another in return, 'What would you like to talk about?' This must be on Page One in the shrink's book of rules. Never give a straight answer. 'What do you think?' is his number two classic question. Also, 'Do you think that was appropriate?' That word 'appropriate' comes up a lot.

One day he asked if I thought it was appropriate to hassle my maths teacher. I looked at Noel as if he was an escapee from a funny farm. But then I said politely, 'No, it probably wasn't appropriate.' It had been a joke, really, just some harmless fun Greta and I had with some others during a Friday afternoon last period. I only mentioned it to pass the time and now I was being quizzed on it, as if there's some dark meaning behind every little thing I do. And so I sat there keeping mum, thinking what was the use.

Noel and I sit and look at one another a lot, like we're playing this game of who's going to be the first to break the ice. Usually he wins. Gotcha, Sophie! But I don't mind. I kind of like getting stuff off my chest. Some stuff, not all of it. There's nobody I trust that much.

Today I take a careful look around his office. On the wall facing me are some colourful prints with patterns on them – very pretty. On the desk near his leather seat stands a box of tissues – expensive ones, impregnated with aloe vera (for patients who like to cry, I suppose), and a travelling clock with its back to me. Sometimes there's a packet of throat lozenges.

Honey and lemon. Above Noel's desk near the door hangs a calendar with a black and white photo of a small boy and girl kissing. I love that picture! His desk is strewn with lots of books and papers.

'What are you thinking of, Sophie?' Noel asks halfway into our session when neither of us has said a word.

'I like the kaleidoscope patterns in your pictures.'

'And why is that?'

The man's a quiz master of the highest calibre.

'I don't know. I just like them.'

'And what else do you like?'

'As in things in this office?'

He shrugs, which I take to mean is what do I like anywhere; in his office, or in the world.

I say the first thing that comes into my head. 'I like ice-cream.'

'What flavour?'

'Liquorice.'

He smiles, glances at the clock when he thinks I'm not watching.

'Do you like ice-cream?' I ask.

This is like tennis. Lobbing the questions back and forth.

'What do you think?'

'I suppose so. I haven't met anyone yet who didn't like it.'

And so it goes on. Don't know why I bother. Or what he gets out of it all.

Sometimes, when I feel like it, I talk about school. Or living with Matt and Amy. Or other people I hang with, like Greta. When I do this, Noel leans forward. As if what I'm saying is fascinating.

'Amy can be pretty out there,' I tell him.

Noel nods. Smiles. 'Yes?'

'I've seen her shoplift.'

I know this is not what the Department pays my shrink a huge packet for – to listen to me gossip about my second-favourite flatmate. But it's easier than talking about myself.

'You want to tell me more?'

I stop short of mentioning her smoking pot and driving without a licence. Funny how the mind works. I think of Amy being in trouble and that lights up a memory of when I was at the Pattersons, my old fosters. Always in hot water there. Without much effort at all I can still see old man Patterson coming at me, about to give me a tongue-lashing.

Noel's voice is somewhere in the background but I'm in another space. Images now zap about my brain – of headless beings, of my younger face, contorted, tearful, lost, of being pulled away screaming from loving arms. Of wolves ripping into me. Then I'm falling into a deep chasm, arms and legs flaying the black and sticky air, and I'm just falling, endlessly falling.

'What are you thinking of, Sophie?'

His voice jolts me back to reality.

'Oh nothing, nothing really.'

Instead of letting Noel anywhere near my deepest feelings, I start rambling on, spitting out whatever wanders into my mind . . . 'And then this dick of a teacher tells her she's on detention. But Greta tells him to shove it and she's off out of there, yelling that he can stick his bloody geography up his . . .'

I am suddenly aware of Noel's hands, small and plump, resting in his lap like delicate white birds.

'You've got little hands,' I say. 'For a man.'

Suddenly the shrink changes, becomes real. A flush shoots up his neck and onto his face. He looks like one of those characters in a kids' puppet show, with beady glass eyes and shiny cheeks the colour of ripe tamarillos.

'Oh, I'm sorry, I didn't mean to be rude or anything. It's just . . .'

He's back in control. Leans forward again. 'Does it worry you that you might have offended me?'

'No. Why would it?'

He waits expectantly as if he knows I've got more to say. Maybe I have, but not this time. Now my mind clangs shut, as does my mouth, my big fat mouth.

6

*M*att's rattling around in the kitchen when I arrive home.

'Hi!'

'Hi, yourself. Want a cuppa?'

'Yeah, thanks.'

By now Matt knows how I like my coffee: white, strong, two sugars. I watch him potter about, getting out the mugs and pouring milk. He flicks a long honey-coloured strand of hair from his eyes.

'Hmm,' he says, studying my face. 'You don't look too good, anything wrong?'

'No, not really. I've just come from seeing Freudie Babe.'

Matt places the mug in front of me and grins.

I like him a lot; I'm even starting to think of him as my best friend. Maybe one day I should tell him . . . He doesn't talk all that much, especially when Amy's with us, but he's thoughtful, perceptive. I think we know each other pretty well now.

He blows on his coffee to cool it. 'They always want to dig inside your brain, those doctors . . .'

'Absolutely.'

'You know, when Mum and Dad and Jenny were killed . . .' He gulps. Those words are still hard to say. 'Well, they took me to a shrink.'

I pet Persia as I wait for him to continue. Matt often pauses between sentences as if he needs to have some control over his thoughts. Or perhaps it is his feelings.

'I suppose I wasn't ready. Refused to say anything about the accident, about the funeral, how I felt. Didn't say a single word.'

'Good for you.'

'Five sessions we sat there. The place had a really nice ceiling . . . and the patterns on the carpet were good too.'

'So what did he say?'

'Nothing much. Although it was a she, actually. Doctor Joy, can you believe?'

'What a hoot!'

Matt's face lights up. 'Yeah. It was funny. Doctor Joy . . . man, was she hot! I tell you, it was very hard to concentrate on what she was saying. Let's just say there were some big distractions . . .'

We both laugh. Then he sits in silence, thinking back to those days, maybe to his family. I watch his fingers – slender and elegant – stroke the side of his mug as he stares into space. We each took different roads to get here, but we're still in the same place, owning the same kind of scars, feeling the same kind of hurt.

'Feel like a hug?' I say it softly. It surprises me as much as him.

'A hug? Yeah, that sounds pretty good.'

There's such a wistful look on his face that my heart clenches. I wrap myself around him. He holds me loosely, his arms looped around my back. There's nothing passionate going on here – neither of us game enough to plunge into deeper water but there's a closeness that I've rarely known. Matt doesn't say anything, just keeps holding me. I wonder if I should reach my face up to his and kiss him. All I have to do is move a fraction of an inch . . . but I can't.

'We should clean the kitchen,' I hear myself say over his shoulder. 'It's disgusting, all this junk.'

'Um, yes.' He breaks away from me. 'Okay. I'll help you.'

We carry on as if nothing has happened, but we know it has. My heart is going *glump*, *glump*, *glump* and I have to sit down.

Later, when he leaves for soccer training, I go back into my room, and put on my CD of *Three Men and a Gun*. I give myself a serve for being chicken. *You idiot! So weak*! But there will be another time for me and Matt – I have to believe that. I lie awake for ages before sleep claims me.

The front doorbell rings and I spring out of bed. It's Jan. She comes around once a week to see how we're coping and early on, when I moved in, she spent a lot of time with me, talking and chilling – really listening, especially one day when I was feeling particularly low. Other welfare people I've known were snobby or nosy or plain apathetic, but Jan breezes in exuding energy, always cheerful and seeming to be genuinely interested in us. Not like Marie who couldn't care less. And Jan always brings something with her, not just her bright, friendly self, but a gift – sometimes a bunch of flowers, a home-cooked cake, some incense. She's special.

Today Jan has news that makes her face light up. She's taking long-service leave to travel overseas.

When she announces this, my hands begin to shake.

'I'm going to India with my friend Nancy.' She does a little hop as she says India. 'I've wanted to go there ever since we studied the country at school. We're backpacking for some of the way.' She pulls out a map and points out the route she and her friend will be taking. I imagine her in baggy shorts and strong hiking boots with a bulging pack on her back – a million miles from care. And me.

'Would you like a cuppa?' I offer, aching for her to stay longer. 'I'd love to hear more about your trip.'

My hands continue to tremble. As I pour the milk, it splatters onto the sink. 'Damn! Sorry!' I drop the cup. It splinters across the floor and hot tea splashes everywhere.

Diving to pick up the broken shards, I wipe a tear

from my cheek. Jan sees it.

'Are you all right, Soph?'

'Yeah, sure.' I manage to smile. 'Just clumsy.'

When the mess is cleared and a new cup is poured, we sit on the back porch and eat the zucchini and raisin cake I made yesterday. Jan is full of the trip and her plans, her long friendship with Nancy, another trip in the future, possibly to Europe. She has no idea how it hurts me.

'Well, my love,' she says some time later, 'I could easily spend hours sitting here with you, but —' She stands and stretches. 'I really have to get back to work.'

I smile, but obviously not all that convincingly, because Jan peers at me with concern. 'You'll be fine with my replacement, won't you, Soph?'

'Of course.' I wave a finger at her, keeping up the jolly act. 'But don't you be gone for too long, will you? I might miss you.'

My voice betrays me as I say that. It cracks. Just a little, but enough for Jan to notice.

'Silly thing. I'm coming back, you know.'

'You better.'

At the front door she hugs me and I feel like they are Arlene's arms around me; Arlene who promised she would always be there for me.

When Jan has gone, I wander around the house, rearranging ornaments, adjusting pictures on walls, and tidying up. I feel adrift. I need to touch familiar objects. I wish I had someone to talk to, to keep me together, but Amy's away for the day and Matt's late home. My stomach's twisted and knotted. I'm happy for Jan and her well-deserved vacation, but I hate the thought of her being gone and maybe never coming back. Sure, she said she would, but what else could she say? I'll miss her so much.

I'm in the bathroom. Thoughts and feelings of again being abandoned are spinning in my head. Round and round. Out of control. Why do people always leave me? Why did my mother leave? Arlene? Dutch? Everyone I have ever cared for. Gone.

In the mirror I watch as I drop my sarong to the floor and survey my milk-white breasts with their pale, strawberry-pink nipples. This body in front of me belongs to someone else. All I have is a mind, mobbed with volcanic, insane thoughts that need to be tamed. There is only one way to do this. The razor.

The blade rests its silver-sharp edge on my flesh, on the soft inside of my forearm near old, faint scars. Inside my head the jumble intensifies. Images surface. Dutch stroking my head for the last time. My hand clasped in his. Arlene smothering my neck with kisses, soft yet indelible. Then she is leaving too. Waving goodbye from a taxi window.

And now the blade is pressing, slicing into the skin. Leaving a thin crimson trail. Pearls of blood. And I am watching, detached. My mind is moving into a place of peace. Peace without pain.

The hand flicks in all directions, creating roads that intersect. Roads long and definite that lead to nowhere. Roads like my life. Without beginning. Without destination.

There. It's done.

I stare in the mirror at the trails, mesmerised as they swell into claret-red, beaded strings. A stranger stares back at me. Her arms are cut and she's bleeding.

We keep watching one another, savouring these brief moments of freedom. She and I are connected by the cuts.

Finally I step out of the dream state. The world is real again and there's a stinging sensation. It's a pain more bearable than having to deal with the chaos in my mind. Even if only for a short time, my anxiety is gone. I'm in control.

Dabbing the blood, I watch it soak into the tissue, spreading. Then I dress in clean clothes and wind a handkerchief around my arm to hide my secret.

In my room I sit with eyes closed and focus on the pain, listen to the breeze outside slapping a bush against the window. When my mind is settled, the crazy thoughts banished, I go into the kitchen for a mug of warm milk and a slice of cake, before heading off to clean the house.

7

After school one day Greta invites me over to her place. It's not wild and chaotic as I'd imagined. Instead, it's clean and neat and comfy. Crocheted rugs, patch-worked wall hangings, and photos of family and friends in frames adorn every ledge and table. It's a home that's loved.

Greta is like a string bean, long and thin. Now I meet her mother for the first time – and she's short and dumpy with burnt-grey hair in need of a cut.

'Sophie, meet Dragon Lady. Grrrr!' Greta drapes herself around her mother's shoulders, grinning and chuckling.

'I'll Dragon Lady you,' her mum replies, the affection between them obvious. 'Call me Daisy,' she says. 'Good to meet you, Sophie.' She hugs me and then grimaces. 'Sorry, I forgot I had flour on my hands.'

'Oh, so have I,' says Greta. She takes delight in slapping my backside to cover me in flour marks.

'Watchit, you,' I snarl, but I'm not angry and Greta knows it.

'Behave yourself!' Daisy scolds. 'She's such a menace, Sophie.'

A pang of envy stabs at me. It would be so good to have this kind of relationship – so good to have a mum.

'I'm going to make you a drink,' Daisy calls as she waddles off to the kitchen. 'Would you like some biscuits with it?'

'No biscuits, Mum.' Greta winks at me. 'Just bring in a bottle of bourbon.'

'In your dreams,' Daisy calls back.

I wander over to check out a photo of the whole family on the wall, two beaming parents with three clear-eyed children smiling angelically, and then there's Greta, no blue and red hair but still playing up for the camera, cross-eyed, her face wreathed in laughter.

'Come and listen to the best music in the world.' Greta grabs my hand and guides me down the hall to her room.

The great divide between my life and hers hits me, crushes me. Everything seems so simple for her, so definite. She's happy and confident. I see the same contentment in her at school. It bubbles out of her like spring water. And she seems so uncomplicated. I'm sure that Greta never mulls over matters as I do until her head is jammed so tightly that it feels as though it's going to explode. That's a world she doesn't even know exists. I could never tell her about the grudges I harbour, the hurts and anxieties that eat away at me like acid. But I can put on the act of being like her today – I lap it up. We veg out to-gether on the floor, music blaring, her loving mum hovering about. But behind the facade I see myself in the mirror, slashing until there is nothing left but a bloodied mess.

'How do you eat that stuff?' Amy shuffles into the kitchen, kimono hanging loosely from her shoulders; tie adrift to reveal her black bikini knickers. Morn-ings are not her best time. I wave my pan with its slices of ham and gooey egg under her nose.

'Yeuk! Take it away!' cries the do-gooder of the animal world, whose main diet is rice crackers and anything coloured green or orange. She pours boiling water into the diffuser and then goes hunting for lite soy milk, muesli and dandelion tea: she's so healthy it's sick. Well, apart from the occasional joint, that is. No one's perfect.

I flip my greasy food onto a plate piled with slices of bread and sit at the kitchen table. Now Amy sits down in front of me and frowns. I've heard it before. 'Why on earth do you eat that crap? White bread! You'll die of cancer, girl.' She doesn't say those exact words this morning but I hear them just the same as she looks at me, rolling her eyes in disgust. We sit for a while, me reading a rock magazine someone's left on the table, she sighing every now and then as life seeps into her dreary morning body.

'Hey, gang.' It's Matt, dressed in his work clothes,

his hair damp from the shower. Amy grumps a reply, I look up and smile with a lift of my lips and eyebrows. He slaps a few doors around, clashes dishes, drops a piece of crockery and swears, and then we are three around the table, happy campers.

'So,' says Matt, 'I'm off to work, and you lucky buggers are bludging, I suppose.'

Amy's too intent on chewing every skerrick of her muesli to bother answering. But I'm not letting him get away with it. 'Well, if you call spending hours getting the groceries and then slaving away in a library writing an English essay bludging, so okay I'm bludging.' I don't tell him that I've also pencilled in chocolate fudge ice-cream and a ten-tissue movie.

'Fair enough,' he says, backing away and grinning as though there's a wicked thought brewing. Then the thought emerges. 'Just so long as I come home to a spotless house with my dinner on the table.'

Amy almost chokes on her muesli. I jump up, grab at a broom and swing it in the general direction of his silly head, both of us laughing.

'Did I say something wrong?' he asks as he disappears out the door. 'Bye!'

'You're a moron,' Amy calls. 'Grow up!' She turns to me and mutters, 'He's so immature.'

'Yeah,' I say. 'Just hopeless.'

We both shake our heads, and smile.

After breakfast, Amy offers to help me with the grocery shopping.

'Sure,' I say. 'That'd be nice.'

We take our time dressing, and a while later dawdle down the street to the shopping centre.

'Actually, I was thinking of taking in a movie,' I confess as we approach the cinema.

'Tell me it's that love saga set in India.' Amy's eyes are alight, and when I nod, she whoops. We check out the session time, and find that *True Obsession* isn't on for another twenty minutes.

'Let's leave the shopping till after, and wait in the park,' she suggests. So we sit on the grass, Amy with her skirt tucked into her knickers and me in shorts, exposing our legs to the sun, watching Saturday afternoon passers-by.

'I'm going to get a navel ring.' Amy pats her tummy. 'My mother had one. Hey, maybe we can get one together.'

'Nah. Not really my scene,' I say. Then I quickly steer the conversation away from me. 'Your mum a bit of a wild child, was she?'

'You could say that.' She smiles, almost in a sad way. 'Mum and my little brothers – Thorn and Harley – we mostly lived wild.'

I laugh, but she continues in earnest. 'Who knows where my dad was? – Mum never talked about him. We lived in this bush camp way out of town, in a sort of hippy commune.'

This explains a lot about Amy: the way she dresses, her habit of leaving her belongings everywhere, the fact that she has no concern about having lights on all day, or leaving the house unlocked when she goes out.

'We grew our own vegies – no chemicals, like really organic, Soph. Good healthy food. And we made our own bread. There were about three families, single women with kids, and we got on really well.' Amy flips onto her stomach and hoists up her skirt for the sun to do its tanning.

I ask, 'What about school?'

'There was none. I mean, we could all read – Mum made sure of that. She was always reading to us. We got by.'

'What was she like? Your mum?'

Amy tears out a tuft of grass. She's in her little space. Can't be reached.

'Sorry,' I say. 'Forget I asked.'

She turns and smiles wryly at me. 'No, that's okay. I can handle it.'

It takes a moment more for her to gather her thoughts.

'So you want the story of my life . . . okay.' Amy's head droops and I can't see her face. 'Well, my mother was a good person, but she did weird, sometimes freaky things.'

She squeezes her eyes shut, fighting back tears. I don't know whether or not to comfort her, but I hate people 'helping' me when I'm upset, so I say nothing.

'She used to get really off her face,' she continues. 'Not drunk or drugged, just out of it – mental problems, I guess. This one time she was so bad I talked her into seeing a doctor. Real clever idea, that. We got into town and he tried to convince Mum she was schizophrenic and needed to take medication. She just laughed at him.' Amy picks at some fluff on her jacket for the longest time. 'Anyway, some welfare people came out to our camp not long after that and took us all to a women's refuge. That's when Mum really lost the plot – got paranoid, imagined bad people were coming after her. That night she took my brothers and disappeared . . . The story of my life – ta da!'

I want to hug her but Amy doesn't give me a chance. Abruptly she's on her feet and striding away.

'Must be time to see that movie,' she says. 'You coming?'

I know how painful it can be when you've stood naked and shown your scars. I tag along behind her without speaking.

When the movie comes out there's still a healthy slice of day left. The sun is gentle and so is the breeze; perfect garden weather. I decide to leave my assignment for the time being.

Back home again, Amy plants herb seeds, and I stare at weeds, trying to scare them away. I'd pull them out but that would mean I'd have to get out

53

of my lovely, peaceful hammock. We chat a while before I say, 'Got a hard question for you, Amy. You up for it?'

'You know me. Up for anything. Ask away.'

'Well, I was wondering . . . how come your mother didn't take you with her?'

'Wish I knew, Soph.' She kneels in front of me, brushing hair out of her face. 'Maybe she thought I was too old to be carted around the countryside. Maybe she just didn't think at all. Keeps me awake sometimes, trying to work it out.' She shrugs. 'What can you do?'

'Then you got fostered, I suppose?'

'Sure did.' She drives a fork into the dirt and un-earths a clump of weeds. 'Some genius decided to put me with the most boring middle-class family they could find.'

'That would have gone down well with you.'

'Oh yeah. Big time. The Browns handed me back just in time. Another day and I would have burnt down their house.'

'I know the feeling.'

'Yep. And then the same genius gave me all the M families – Murphy, Mitchell, Morrison – I hate Ms! And then it was the Dawsons – hopeless! And finally some nice Greeks. That didn't work because we couldn't understand each other. I'd swear at them and they'd smile. Where's the fun in that?'

'Did you ever find out what happened to your mum?'

'No. She's just gone . . .'

'Hellooo. Anyone home?'

I see a face peering over the side fence. It's Jan. I run to open the gate but halfway there force myself to slow down. I can't let her see how much she means to me.

'Hi, Sophie.' I get a warm smile. She and Amy, who stays in the garden, exchange waves.

'It's so good to see you, Jan.' I hear myself gushing and try to tone it down. 'You going to stay for a coffee?'

'No, I can't this time, sweetie. Have to catch a plane – the big trip begins today!'

She almost bounces with joy. Her eyes gleam. I'm glad to see her happy but that feeling is smothered by another. She's leaving me. Still, I smile along with her, my mask firmly in place.

Jan explains she only dropped in to do her duty: tell us her replacement's name, say an official goodbye. I knew that was the reason for her visit, but still it hurts me to hear it from her. Moments later I feel okay again. Transported out of my misery into bliss. And all because she hugs me, squeezing the cuts hidden under my jumper, making me feel alive.

'Now you take care of yourself, eh, Sophie?'

'I will, Jan. Come back soon, won't you?'

'Be back before you know it. You keep safe now.'

I want to hug her again but I just stand there, rigid. She puts a hand on my shoulder. 'You okay?'

'Couldn't be better,' I say. 'Perfect.'

8

*F*or days after Jan's visit, my thinking is chaotic and irrational; I can't concentrate at school and my sleep is restless. Matt comes into my room one night and I shriek when I find him standing over me, his hand reaching for me.

'You were having a nightmare,' he says quietly. I remember that and nothing else as I fall back asleep straight away. It's not a restful sleep. I wake again and again, terrified by my dreams.

'Something was really upsetting you last night,' Matt says at the breakfast table. 'What was going on?'

'I can't remember,' I say, shrugging.

Amy shuffles into the kitchen. 'What're you two talking about?'

'Nothing,' we answer in unison.

In today's session Noel has finally taken the initiative and asked me a definitive question. He wants to know what I plan to do with my life.

'Become a shrink,' I reply. 'So I can torture people.'

Something about that answer tickles him and he grins. 'Do you think that's what I do, Sophie?'

'You try sitting here,' I say.

After that we slip into the world of silence. Ten minutes of mental chess goes by and neither player blinks. Finally boredom gets to me.

'We're studying Political Science at school. Politics interests me. Might try that as a career choice.' I don't mean it. It's just something to say. I like to confuse him when I can. 'About being a shrink, I was only joking.'

He nods and purses his lips, which is one of his few facial expressions during our sessions.

Encouraged by his response, I talk about school, the subjects I'm studying and a little about the group I hang with. They're not bad girls, really, but they don't back down easy, and all of us are feminists.

'Not man-hating feminists,' I point out, just in case he was wondering. 'Not the sort who burn their bras and want to cut off men's balls.'

I said that for effect and it worked. A nerve twitches on Noel's forehead. The mind-flash I have of my shrink reaching down to cover his privates causes me to laugh. Can't miss an opportunity like this.

'Not that they don't deserve it,' I add.

'Mm,' comments Noel. And I think to myself, '*Checkmate!*'

That night I have another one of my dreams. I'm

tumbling into a bottomless gorge in slow motion. This merges into a scene where I view the world as if from a vast distance. There are no clear edges to anything. Colours take on a grimy appearance; everything is brushed with the same shade of grey – sky, grass, people. As I move, I feel as though I'm automated and that parts of my body – my hands and fingers, legs and chest – belong to someone else. When I speak, the words echo as if in a chamber. Everything about me exists in another time and place. I wake in a lather of sweat.

The next day I carry the dream with me. All through my classes I trip in and out. Physically I'm sitting in front of my easel in the art room painting a rural landscape, but my mind is riding to another place. It's an unsettling feeling. Much of the time I don't dare to close my eyes for fear of dreams, and now they pursue me in the daylight.

At lunchtime I hear Greta's voice, loud and commanding. 'She's been cutting herself.'

How could she know about it? How could she tell people? I'm about to run when someone asks Greta who she's talking about.

My heart double-beats.

'Hayley Evans,' Greta answers. 'That pretty new girl. She must be an idiot.'

I move closer, making sure as I do that the sleeves of my jumper are pulled down to cover my own scars.

Cassie steps into the discussion. 'That's not fair, Greta,' she says. 'You can't just judge her like that without knowing the facts.'

'The fact is she's dumb. Why would anyone want to cut themselves up?' Greta looks around at us, demanding an answer. Her eyes stop at me.

'What do you think, Soph?'

'I have no idea . . . unless it makes her feel good.'

'Are you mad? How could cutting yourself feel good?'

My shoulders slump. I want to disappear.

'I don't know,' I say lamely.

Someone points out Hayley, standing near the canteen.

'I'm going to set her straight,' Greta says.

She strides away before I can stop her. But I know deep down that I really don't have the courage to speak up. I hate myself for that.

'I know other girls who cut themselves,' Cassie tells me. 'It's not like Greta thinks – they're not dumb.'

If I say anything I'll draw attention to myself, so I shrug and change the subject.

Later I think about finding Hayley and comparing notes. But the coward in me re-emerges. She has her demons, I have mine. We must each face them on our own.

9

*F*or weeks now I've been dreading today. Marie has come to take me for a case conference review. This is a reminder, in case I ever dare forget it, that, much as I want it, my life isn't yet my own. The Department will put me under its microscope like I'm an insect as its team of arrogant fools poke and prod me with questions, to check my 'progress', or lack of it. The aim of the exercise is for them to decide if I should be allowed to continue living independently. What I want doesn't matter.

Marie raps on the door, short, crisp and business-like. That sums her up in every way. If she has any warmth in her, she leaves it at home when she goes to work.

'Oh.' It's obvious from the moment she sees me that she doesn't approve of what I'm wearing. 'I thought you'd be in your school clothes.' She pats her hands on either side of her suit jacket, as though she needs to brush something sticky from them.

'No,' I say brightly. 'This is how I usually dress for school.' Amy has lent me a long Indian skirt that swishes when I walk and almost touches my sandals. I rattle my mass of bangles, just to annoy Marie, and flash a smile to rub it in.

'Very well . . . do you think you'll be all right this morning? I wouldn't want you to get upset. That does no one any good.'

Once I totally lost it at a case conference. Swore at Marie. Swore at the whole bunch of Department suits. They kept pushing me to live with this couple I hated: it was nothing personal – I hated everyone then.

'I'm fine,' I tell her. 'Let's just get it over with.'

We drive ten blocks in silence, and then, because it must be Department policy, Marie asks a question.

'How are your sessions going with Doctor Palmer?'

'Okay.'

'And school?'

'Okay.'

She can waste her words if she wants but I'm not wasting mine. I know that in her briefcase are reports from my school, and from Noel. There's probably one from Jan, too. She'll have them all neat and tidy in a folio to hand over at the conference. I hate this.

Marie checks her make-up in the rear-vision mirror, rubs at her bottom lip to smooth some lipstick and pats a stray hair into place. 'Anything you want to tell me?' she says. She rarely uses my name when she's addressing me. Around her colleagues she acts differently. I'm Sophie then, and she has nothing but the utmost concern for my welfare. Makes me sick.

'No,' I reply. 'I've got nothing to tell you.'

She persists, as she always does.

'No problems with your flatmates?'

I beam the cheeriest smile I can muster. 'No, Miss Jarmine, I couldn't ask for two nicer people to live with.'

'You realise we've only put you there on a trial basis?' Marie seems to enjoy telling me this – such power. 'When you talk to Mr Donovan, I want you to answer him as fully as you possibly can. If you hope to keep living where you are, you'll need to create a good impression. I have to stress this – if we can't see that you're making a genuine effort to co-operate with your psychiatrist, and with your school, then it's quite possible that you could be placed in fostering again. You understand that, don't you?'

I want to cut. A vision of a sharp blade on my skin trailing a bloodied line skates through my mind.

'Yes.' I force myself to speak. 'I do understand. I've been working hard. Doctor Palmer and I are making real progress.'

She turns and smiles falsely. 'That's good, dear. If you're on your best behaviour this morning I'm sure there won't be any problems.'

I smile back at her, just as falsely.

Last month I carved my initials into my arm. It was up high where I could hide it with clothing. Over the weeks the wound dried, scabbed, and then the scab came off until all that remained was a faint white scar. The feeling I had when I did it stays with me, bright red and vivid in my mind. I like the pain of cutting. I like too that my body has my own brand of tattoo carved on it, and no matter how much I am documented and dissected, this is a piece of me that no one owns. Marie and the others who control my life know nothing. They can't manipulate it. They can't take it away. It's mine. Just mine.

The car stops in front of an electronic gate. It opens and we drive into the underground car park. 'You don't need to be nervous,' Marie says. She always babbles this before a case conference as if it's part of a memorised script. We drive into a space marked *Reserved*.

'Oh, I forgot to tell you, Rosemary Stewart asked me to give you this letter.' She hands me a white envelope with my name written on the front in a familiar script. 'It'd be nice if you replied to her.'

I drop the letter into my bag. First chance I get I'll throw it, unopened and unread, into the nearest rubbish bin. The Stewarts gave me away. Like all the others.

We walk to the meeting, Marie leading, and, like Shakespeare's schoolboy, I follow *creeping like snail, unwillingly*.

The conference room. A big table. Chairs all around

63

it. Open blinds on the windows. Light in my eyes. Nothing on the walls to check out.

I wait alone while Marie meets outside with her colleagues, their voices too indistinct to make out what they're saying about me. I've been at case conferences more times than I care to remember. They are always the same – as awful as it gets.

Hurry up, you morons.

The door swings open. In troop the heavies, sombre-faced. Marie follows them. There's been a Departmental shuffle and except for Marie these are new people sitting opposite. They look at me like I'm some zoo animal that's expected to perform on cue.

'This is Sophie.' My case worker wears a smile like tacky wallpaper. 'Sophie, this is Mr Donovan. He's in charge of proceedings.'

Big boss. Big baboon.

'And Mr Alexander is a new housing outworker here, taking over from Miss Jones. You don't mind if he sits in?'

As if I have any option.

'And this is Ms Matherson who's going to take minutes of our little meeting.'

I feel like asking what their Christian names are. After all, I've only been introduced as Sophie. But that's just one of the many rebellious feelings I have. Like the others, I have to nail this feeling down while I nod respectfully as each suit is introduced. They nod back in turn, inspecting me briefly before referring to papers in front of them.

The secretary hands me a typed agenda and I bury my face in it.

'As you know,' Marie drones, 'Sophie was placed in a share accommodation situation some time ago. She lives with two other young people. The details are on page one of your folders.'

All eyes go down to the report and the meeting crawls through more red tape, until Marie flips through a thick folder – my case notes.

Putting on her glasses, she says, 'I'll just give a quick briefing of Sophie's history, leading up to the present day.'

I'm not sure whether to laugh or cry.

Eight minutes later. 'So, as you see, it hasn't always been easy for our girl; she's been through a lot of fostering.'

Our girl? That makes me cringe.

They trot out the usual questions: 'How are you?'

'Have you settled in well?'

'How are you coping at school?'

'Would you say your current situation is preferable to being fostered with a family?'

Nobody's listening to my answers, not really. I know how to fix that.

We have wild parties. Orgies. You should come and join us.

I flirt with saying it for a second, until Marie's glare cuts me down.

'So what do you think are the benefits of shared accommodation for you?'

'There are so many good things about it,' I say. I can play their game, know all the right buttons to press. 'I'm learning how to budget, how to get on with guys my own age, and I can study in peace . . .'

They're flipping through reports, looking at watches – must be time for a coffee break soon.

'I hope I can stay where I am.' I finish there and glance hopefully around the table. That's as close to begging as I intend to go.

They don't respond, of course.

Marie passes a folder to each of them.

'This is a report from the therapist, Doctor Palmer.'

I'm put on hold as they flick through the pages. They couldn't possibly be reading them. Probably looking for some part that's underlined or in capitals. Maybe they're searching for the word PSYCHO.

They won't get much from Noel's report. I haven't said anything to him that's even the tiniest bit in-criminating. I look at the carpet as they read, but I feel their eyes every time they move from the report to me, as if they're searching for some dark secret that Noel has missed.

'I see,' murmurs Donovan when he finishes reading.

That's all the feedback I get. I drum my fingers on the table. I'd like to punch a wall, but I adjust my face and continue to sit there, looking as demure as I possibly can.

Next is Marie's report. It's mercifully brief because she has no idea who I am. After that, Donovan and Alexander put their heads together to compare dates in diaries and then all the folders around the table are closed.

'That's it, young lady.' Donovan smiles at me. It's the kind of expression a walrus has when overseeing its harem. 'Didn't hurt, did it?'

Yuck.

I respond with a wan smile and a shake of my head.

'Good girl,' Marie says. 'You did very well.'

One day, I tell myself, one day it won't be like this.

10

'Well, here we are!' Marie exclaims, as if we have suddenly materialised out of thin air. We're parked in front of my school.

'Thanks.' I gather my things.

She can't resist one last lecture. 'They'll review again, as you know, so living with your young friends is still subject to change. It's all in your hands. If you do the right thing . . .'

'Yep. Got it.' I step out of the car.

'No, I don't think you do have. You should appreciate how lucky you are to be in your present situation.'

'I appreciate it. Okay? What more do you want me to say?'

Marie leans across and closes the door on me, ending the conversation, and then infuriates me by smiling. 'Take care, dear,' she says through the open window.

All pretence stops then, on my part anyway. She waves at me as she drives off. I stare after her. As soon as she is around the corner, I make a decision.

No way can I face school. At home I change into my bathers and T-shirt. I wrap a bandage around my still raw wounds and when I'm done, wheel Matt's bike onto the road.

It's an overcast day and the pool is occupied by only three people, all swimming laps in the grey, chilled water. I take up the far lane. The water really stings the cuts on my arms and I feel like getting out. But I've come to swim. It's the best way I know to calm my churning mind. However, almost as soon as I launch off and get into my stride, thoughts jostle for attention. Jerky and fragmented. Nightmarish thoughts. Cutting my skin, slicing off the flesh, making mounds of it, throwing what remains of myself off a cliff.

I try to focus on being here in the water. Watch as my arms propel past my face and bubbles rise. Count my breaths. In. Out. In. Out. The pastel blue wall, blotched with vast tracts of mould-coloured lichen, passes by. Up, down, in, out, so many thoughts, the razor, the cliff, cutting, cutting . . .

I burst out of the water gasping, but so relieved to see the blue sky, the tranquil blue sky.

When I arrive back at the house and wheel the bike into the hallway, I have no thought other than to crawl into bed and sleep.

'You seem preoccupied today,' Noel observes later that week in our Wednesday afternoon session.

'Where is your mind?'

'In my brain. You should know that, Mister Doctor.'

'Are you tired?' Noel is in his usual pose, leaning slightly forward, elbows on the arms of his chair, making a bridge with his interlocking fingers.

'I am a bit.' I don't tell him that every molecule of blood in my body feels like sludge.

'Have you been sleeping well?'

'Not really.'

'Dreams?'

'Always.'

He doesn't push me. He waits. Unless I volunteer the information, it ends here. And it does.

'Just stupid dreams. Nothing you'd be interested in.'

I don't trust myself to say anything. I don't want him to see what's inside this riotous mind. I relax back into my chair, aware from time to time of his soothing voice, but it's far off. I feel like I'm almost in a hypnotic state. And then he's standing and showing me his kind smile.

'It's time to go, Sophie.'

Already? It went by so quickly . . . I must have been wandering again. I have no idea where I got to.

At home I fall into bed and sleep, so deeply. I wake at the sound of Matt moving around in another room. There's a scary person in the mirror so I try not to look at her as I straighten my hair. Then, my happy face fixed in position, I re-enter the world.

Amy's off somewhere; said she'd be away for a few days.

'Hi, Matt.'

'Hey, Soph. Glad I caught you. Thought you might like to come out with me tonight. I'm going with Tracey and Boyd. We're checking out a new band. You up for it?'

I hesitate. A noisy band, having to make conversation – these are the last things I want right now.

'Come on, Soph. You can bring some friends along if you want.'

Have to try, I tell myself.

'Sure,' I say. 'I'd love to.'

I SMS Greta and she is back to me within moments.

I'm in, meet u there

The air is sticky-hot, stifling even. I feel so stupid throwing on a jacket in this weather, but I have things to hide. Matt looks as though he's going to comment, but thankfully keeps his thoughts to himself.

'My friend Greta's coming too,' I tell him.

'Excellent!'

The band is in full swing when we get there, the pub loud and crowded with smelly bodies. Tracey and Boyd arrive almost at the same time. The boys head off for beers while Tracey and I find a table and scrounge some chairs. Tracey's full of stories.

She tells them with great excitement but I'm unable to focus on anything she says. The thoughts in my head are screaming – so much turmoil.

'Sophie!' It's Greta. She's dressed in a textured silver mini-skirt, skyscraper-high party shoes, and her boobs are almost hanging out of her low-cut top. 'Well, I'm here,' she says. 'What now?'

Matt turns up at that moment with drinks, takes one look at Greta and gulps. Obviously he likes what he sees. Is it my imagination, or is she leaning slightly forward so he can get a better view of what she's offering? No, it's definitely not my imagination. I'm forgotten as she and Matt slip into an animated conversation, like long-lost friends reunited.

'You want to watch that girl,' Tracey says. 'She's moving fast.'

I laugh it off. 'Doesn't bother me. Good luck to her.'

The music is pounding, drumming loudly in my head to compete with the confusion there.

'Drink up, girls.' Boyd delivers the remaining drinks to our table.

I gulp down my beer. I'm not used to drinking and I don't know what it might do to me. But I intend to find out. I make for the bar and order a shot of tequila – the barman doesn't question my age – put it away fast and order another. The warm, fuzzy feeling that descends upon me settles my mind. I tap my foot and sway with the beat of the music. It's a wild band. A guy comes up, invites me to dance. I go with him but I'm unsteady on my feet. He holds me. 'Take it easy, sweetheart.' Then I'm dancing, losing myself, forgetting that my new best friend is not far away. With Matt. My Matt.

'Hey.' My dance partner's lips are hot against my ear. 'You want to come to my place? I've got much better music there.'

'No!' I jerk away from him.

'Okay. Jesus.' He shoulders past me and disappears into the crowd.

Back at the bar I order a vodka, lime and soda.

'You okay, love?' Tracey asks when I return to my seat.

'Sure.'

Greta's at the table too, sipping some sort of cocktail. I give her a look. She's lucky that's all I give her.

'Matt bought it for me.' She grins. 'You didn't tell me what a spunk he is.'

Spunk. Sunk. Dunk. Drunk. The words swirl around my head. I can see them bobbing up and down like ducks in water. They make me grin.

'You're drunk, girl.' Greta stands, grabs me by my elbow and manoeuvres me towards the Ladies. Once inside, she heads into a cubicle, talking the whole time. 'If Matt's already taken, if you and he have something going, then I'll back off. You just give me the word. But if you don't want him . . .' She prattles on and on.

All I can think is how odd I feel. The ground seems to be moving under my feet, as though I'm

73

on an escalator, going down, down, down. I clutch the hand basin but my legs slip from under me and I land on my bum, find myself sitting on the cold tiles. Cold bum, warm head. It's so funny!

'What are you laughing about?'

Greta comes out of the cubicle, sees me on the floor and bends over, offering me a hand.

'God, Sophie. How much have you had to drink?'

'Just enough!'

For once my teeming fevered brain is full of nothing but bubbles. I feel woozy and suddenly wonderful.

'Come on. Let's get you home.' Greta yanks at me, trying to pull me upright, but I want to stay forever on the cool floor.

Now she's splashing tap water over me.

'Stop it. Leave me alone.'

She ignores me.

'You must be blazing hot in that jacket.'

She kneels down and starts to take it off me.

My words are slurred but still she must be able to understand a 'No!' – a yelled 'No!' It doesn't stop her. She pulls the jacket clear of me and through bleary eyes I see her staring at the cuts and scars on my arms.

'You stupid idiot,' she says. 'You stupid, stupid idiot!'

Her disgusted face is the last thing I remember.

11

I'm deep in the forest, near where I used to live, on a ledge high above a gorge, peering into a dark abyss. The wind is picking up and I'm swaying backwards, forwards, and I know I can't fight it much longer. I'll fall into the blackness and my body will never be found.

It's the next day. I'm sitting in Noel's office, recounting my latest dream. When I stop talking, I dimly recall Tracey and Matt taking me home from the bar last night. I know my jacket was on so Matt didn't see anything. But Greta did. Now she knows my darkest secret.

'Sophie?'

Noel is looking at me intently, as though my mind is a book with pages open wide for him to read.

'You sound deeply unhappy,' he says.

All I want is to be alone. I'm only here because I have to be. I wish the whole world would go away.

'I'm not unhappy.' I drop my head as I say it.

'Are you thinking of harming yourself?'

That starts my mind racing. Why would he ask that? I think of Greta, staring. Maybe she's said something. It could have got back to Noel. I struggle to think how – maybe she told Matt and he . . .

Noel's voice cuts into my thoughts.

'You're not your usual self today.'

'I got smashed last night. My head aches.'

'Why did you drink so much?'

'I don't know.'

'Were you drinking to block out your feelings?'

I shrug. I wish he'd shut up and leave me alone. I try to excise him from my mind, pretend that he doesn't exist.

'I'm worried about you, Sophie.'

My hands automatically cover my eyes.

'I wonder if perhaps you have thoughts of killing yourself.'

I fall back against the chair, shaking my head.

'No. No. No!'

Noel takes a notepad from his desk, and scribbles on it.

'I think it'd be best if you were to go into hospital for a few days. For your own safety.'

I hate him. 'I don't want to go to hospital. Are you saying that because I got drunk? Because of the dream? The dream wasn't real. I made it up. I was lying to you!'

'Yes, the dream is a part of it, Sophie. The drinking. Your general demeanour. I feel that you've been slipping for a while now. It really sounds to me as if you might be planning to . . . to hurt yourself.'

'I'm not planning anything!'

'You're not feeling suicidal again?'

'No.'

'I believe you, but still, for a short while, I think you need to be protected from yourself.'

'Truly, I'm only tired. I haven't been sleeping very well lately. You asked me to talk and that was just some stupid dream I had. Or I think I had. Please don't put me into hospital. I'm getting better all the time. Please.'

'It would be irresponsible of me not to admit you. Given what happened last time. And it is only for a little while.'

I try every argument I can think of but he's not listening anymore. He's on the phone to Marie, betraying me.

I sit there thinking of how when I'd overdosed before, I'd been threatened with a psych hospital. Just the idea of being locked up had terrified me. I'd managed to wriggle out of it then with the compromise that I would see a shrink regularly. And now that shrink – Noel – isn't listening but is making plans to commit me.

Too quickly I'm in Marie's car headed for the hospital. After the first handful of platitudes she doesn't say much. It's all part of the job for her – carting another crazy off to the loony bin.

I am so frightened. What are they going to do to me? Will they lock me in a cell? Will they make me take off my clothes and see my cuts? At that moment the worst thing happens. I cry in front of Marie. Without a word of comfort she passes me a tissue. I throw it on the floor. I close my eyes – I'm so tired – and when I open them I'm in a waiting room filled with mad people. I try to hide from their vacant stares, their hate-the-world eyes. It's a real nightmare this time. Trapped in a room with mad people. And I'm one of them.

'I have to go now,' Marie says. 'I've explained everything to the nurse. She's got Doctor Palmer's referral and I've left my details if you need anything. I'll call by tomorrow to see how you're going.'

Her hand reaches out to me as if some long dormant maternal instinct has been stirred. She pulls it back, the distance between us just too far.

'Don't worry,' she says as she stands to go. 'That's the main thing.'

An hour goes by. I count off each minute. Then a nurse ushers me into a cubicle and leaves me to sit alone until a doctor arrives. He's young with a bristly face as if he's either trying to grow a beard or hasn't had time to shave. 'Now, what seems to be the problem?' He speaks quickly and glances at his watch.

When I took the overdose, the doctor who treated me then was as dismissive as this one. I bet I'm only a number to him.

I refuse to speak.

'The referring doctor seems to believe you're suicidal. Is that how you feel?'

My lips remain gripped together.

'I'll take that as a yes.'

Only cowardice stops me from spitting in his face.

He calls for a nurse as he finishes up his paperwork. While he's distracted I should run. But I can hardly stand. My shoes are made of lead. It's difficult to even think. I want to sleep, sleep, and never wake up.

12

*I*n the psych ward every exit door is locked; every window has iron bars or mesh. I slump in a plastic chair near my bed, too tired to even take off my sandals. A short, pudding of a woman in a chenille dressing gown wanders past, back and forth, talking to herself. She's annoying. After a while, she becomes infuriating.

'Be quiet!' I rasp at her. She ignores me and keeps yabbering. God is warning her that she is to save the world; the Devil will kill all babies; Mary, her mother, is watching her . . .

Inside my mind are demons enough without her constant, crazy babble. There's one part of me that knows I should feel sorry for her. But this place changes you quickly and I hear another, stronger part of me, threatening her.

'If you don't shut up, I'll come and shut your fat gob for you.' It doesn't sound like my voice.

Trying to blot her out, I find the energy to flip off my sandals, strip, pull on a gown and climb into bed. But nothing can blot her out. I put my head under the blankets, press against my ears. Her shrill voice pursues me.

I dive out of bed and storm up to her, shaking her by the shoulders.

'Stop it!'

'God is in charge of my soul! I am His divine instrument!'

'Enough! I told you – enough!'

I slap her face. Hard.

'The Blessed Virgin is amongst us! Oh Mary full of grace . . .'

She stands there raving. Doesn't flinch or try to protect herself. I could hit her again and again, and it wouldn't make any difference. She's not here in this world; she's in her own, damned head space. I feel more ashamed than I've ever been in my life. The poor woman wanders out of the room, proclaiming God and Mary to the walls. Even so, she's more at peace than I am.

Sometimes it feels like there's another person inside of me who takes control. I see myself doing the weirdest things – like attacking that woman, or thinking of self-destructing – and it's as though I'm watching someone else. I can be wildly happy, and hours later in the depths of despair. I'm never in the middle like everyone else. Soaring or falling, that's me.

An orderly rattles by with a metal trolley full of plates, jerking me away from my thoughts to the cold reality of the hospital.

That night they give me pills to sleep and I don't fight it. Oblivion is a good place.

The next day I find I'm in C Ward. Patients are kept here for observation, I'm told. Doctors and nurses, bureaucrats – they all love to observe me. There's nothing much to do. The other patients, older than me, wander around aimlessly or park themselves in chairs in the central courtyard. Some are dressed oddly. Some walk as if in a trance, and no wonder: they're all on meds, doped out of their loopy brains. The demented, religious woman is no longer here, thank goodness.

For the most part I hide out in a deserted chairs-and-whiteboard-only room. For once I have something to be thankful to Marie for. She dropped off some exercise books at the office this morning so I can use one as a journal. It's my magic cape. I twirl it around, and disappear inside it.

In my life all seems frail,
precarious,
emotions fleeting,
relationships fragmentary . . .

'Hello.' A young woman with short, ragged hair stands in front of me.

She gets a cursory nod but I keep writing.

'My name's Lola and I'm on the Patients' Committee. I just wanted to welcome you.'

I don't respond. She takes this as a cue to continue. 'I'm supposed to see that you settle in all right, and if you have any suggestions on how to improve the place.'

'Okay.' I don't lift my eyes to her. Some people can't be fazed, though. And she's one of them.

'I'm here because I wasn't taking my medication so I had a psychotic episode. What are you here for?'

Now I look at her. 'I'm mental.'

She scarcely draws breath. 'No you're not. We've all got problems. Group Therapy's on soon. I find it very helpful for dealing with my troubles.'

I swivel my seat around so that I almost have my back to her, and keep writing. It's rude, but with someone like her, it's either rudeness or a brick.

'Okay then,' she says. 'Well, it's been nice meeting you. I'll see you at Group. Bye for now.'

At last she goes. Great! I can't stand nosy do-gooders. And Group Therapy – I know I'm going to hate that even more.

Twenty minutes later a nurse arrives with bad news. 'Time for Group.'

Fann-tastic!

She ushers me into the Day Room where I become part of a circle of patients – including Lola – who are supposed to talk to one another about whatever is on their minds.

I push my chair back so I'm as far away from

the others as I can be without some nurse hauling me back into line. I don't want to be part of their precious games.

Rachel, a young red-haired nurse, is the Group leader. I keep my eyes focused on the floor as she introduces me to the others. Like trained parrots, they chorus, 'Hello, Sophie.' The floor continues to fascinate me.

The rules of engagement in a group session are simple but she recites them at caterpillar pace, as if she's a pre-school teacher and we're the backward class. One person speaks at a time. No interjections. And most importantly, Rachel declares, 'What is said in Group stays here.'

Yeah, yeah; heard that one before.

Theresa's the first guinea pig. Sallow skin, Coke-bottle glasses. She goes on and on about another patient, Mark, who she says keeps bugging her. 'I don't want anything to do with him. Tell him to leave me alone!'

Rachel looks at Mark.

'What's been happening?' she asks.

He's a stutterer. It's painful to listen as he tries to force out the words. She obviously already knew that before she asked him to speak. She should never have put him on the spot.

With great effort, and humiliation, he says, 'I'm just trying to be friendly.'

'Not with me!' Theresa jumps up and shoots a

finger at him. 'Be friendly with someone else – you freak!'

The others don't seem to mind this exchange. Apparently it's common.

Rachel doesn't blink. 'How do you think we can support both Theresa and Mark with this problem?' she asks the group.

I can't help myself. 'Take a pill,' I say. 'We should all take a lot of pills. That would help.'

My chair goes flying out from behind me and I rack off before anyone can say a word.

I'm left alone after that. They must have put me on the Watch-Out-She's-Trouble list. Cool. No one tries to get me to join in with the table tennis comp in the Day Room. Draughts, chess – no invitations come my way. And I definitely won't be sitting with the couch potatoes watching TV soapies. A few patients wander by, but if they get too close, I try to look dangerous and they leave. I sit for a long time, wanting nothing. I've got this place sussed out.

Just when I think they've forgotten about me, a nurse arrives to tell me I have to see the doctor. Reluctantly, I agree.

The doctor's name is Helen Marshall. She asks how I am. I don't answer.

'What do you think is wrong with you, Sophie?'

I ignore that, too.

'I have a letter from Doctor Palmer. He seems very concerned about you.'

Silence engulfs the room like a huge black cloud.

At last she says, 'Is there anything you want to tell me?'

I watch tree branches thrash in the wind outside, scattering leaves.

'We'll put you in the Adolescent Unit in a day or two. You should feel more comfortable there.'

As I pass her on my way out, she places her hand on my shoulder. 'Take care, my dear.'

The way she says 'dear' is so different to Marie. Like I really matter to her.

In the toilets, hidden from the inquisitive eyes of nurses and patients, I can't stop crying.

After three torturous days I am transferred out of C Ward to the kids' ward. The very act of putting one foot in front of the other takes every drop of my concentration and energy. I don't want to eat or write or read or even breathe. I don't know what's happening to me: everything lacks colour, as if I'm seeing the world through dark wire gauze. All I want is to stay in bed forever, but the nurses – damn them – are constantly trying to jolly me into activity.

There are five others in the unit: Ashley, Emma, Felix, Holden, and Lauren. I haven't responded to any overtures of friendship so they've left me alone. I don't want to tell my life story. Sick to death of that.

In Group, the new therapist, Shelley, keeps asking me questions, but I look straight through her.

Yesterday she asked Lauren a question, but Lauren, my new hero, told her to 'Shut up, bitch-face'. Lauren keeps fighting the staff, abusing them, not doing what they want. If I wasn't feeling so crappy I'd join forces with her.

My sessions with the doctor are getting nowhere. I don't want to talk with her so I retreat into my old pal, Silence. As much as I can I keep my head down; that way I don't need to make any contact. Sometimes I close my eyes and drift off. The doctor said to call her Helen, if I like. She sits, clasping her hands in her lap. They are narrow hands, white and dappled with freckles, which Arlene used to call 'flowers of death'. From time to time she twists a diamond ring on her right hand. Sometimes she tells me about herself. So far I know she's a single mother with a ten-year-old daughter, Cara, and that she went to an all girls' school. Oh yes, and she likes bodysurfing. I think she chatters on to fill the gaps of silence, or perhaps it is to make me feel comfortable with her. Her voice is low and gravelly. She's tall and well-padded. Not fat or even chubby. She's just right. Her hair, the colour of butterscotch, is looped onto her head, held in place with clips. When she walks beside me, escorting me to the door after our sessions, I smell a whiff of her perfume. It's exotic, like white lilies, which I love.

She has put me on antidepressants so now I line up with the others in a conga line of loonies as nurses dole out our medication, a bandaid against demons. I don't really mind it all that much. Maybe I can never beat my demons, but the meds make them quieter than usual.

13

A week passes before Matt comes to visit me. I wasn't expecting anyone, certainly not him, so I'm not properly dressed for his visit. I feel embarrassed that he should see me looking so bedraggled, barefoot and in old jeans. God only knows how bad my hair must look.

'Hey there.' He walks up behind where I sit alone and brooding, and leans over my shoulder, his face so close I can feel his breath on my neck.

'I've missed you,' he whispers.

If it was any other place, I would hug him, but, aware people are watching, I say nothing. Instead, I clench the tissue in my hand and hope I don't start blubbering.

Matt pulls up a chair and sits in front of me. 'Hope you don't mind me visiting. I was here before, when you first arrived – but they wouldn't let me see you.'

'I'm sorry. I probably couldn't have seen anyone then.'

'Not a problem. As long as you're all right. You are, aren't you?'

'Yes. I'm really good. Ready to go home.'

He lays a bunch of flowers in my lap – a cheerful mix of reds and yellows and blues. No guy has ever given me flowers before. I mumble that they are beautiful.

'Aw, Sophie.' He takes my hand. 'I'd give you flowers every day if it made you happy.'

A part of me – my heart? my soul? – crumples like paper in a fire. I cover my face so he can't see what he's done to me.

'It's okay, Soph. Let it out.'

Nurses and patients walk past, staring at this sobbing girl, but I ignore them.

'I didn't realise you were in such a bad way,' he says. 'I would have camped outside the damn door until you were up to seeing me.'

'There was nothing you could have done.'

'Yeah, there was. I could have stayed with you.' He holds my hand even tighter.

He stays with me until way past visiting hours. The nurses leave us alone – there's not even a gentle hint. It's so good to have news from beyond the hospital walls. And Matt is happy to do the talking while I soak it in.

I discover that he and Amy have cleaned our house from top to bottom. 'You'd never recognise the place!'

And Amy has a new boyfriend – with dreadlocks and body piercings.

'That's why she hasn't been in to see you,' Matt explains. 'She's always out with this Johnny guy – but she will come visit soon. She misses you, same as I do. And old Persia misses you a real lot.'

I nod. 'Yeah, because I'm the one who never forgets to feed him.'

'True,' Matt says. 'He's a smart pussycat, Persia.'

Not once does he ask what I'm doing in this place. I'm so grateful.

Then he comes out with the most surprising news of all.

'Greta rang.'

'What did you tell her?'

'That you were in hospital.'

'Oh . . . did she say anything?'

'Only that she hopes you're well soon. And she sent her love.'

Tears well up in my eyes again. I was so sure that Greta would not want anything to do with me, not after she'd found out I was cutting myself.

Matt touches my cheek. 'Tell me true. You okay?'

I take his hand and kiss it. It's not a sexual thing. It's me telling him all the things I can't find words for.

'Yes,' I mutter. 'I'm okay.'

When he leaves, I keep a picture of him in my mind for a long while after. It's so good to know I'm not completely alone.

A week later and colours are brighter. Things don't seem all leached out now, and though I continue to feel sluggish, I have more energy. Helen asks if I'm feeling better and I nod. It's the first time in days that I have responded to her in any way.

'That's good, Sophie,' she tells me. 'I'm pleased.'

I want to look at her, but I feel . . . I don't know what, shy isn't really the right word; stubborn maybe. If I look at her, I might be compelled to talk. And talking with a shrink is the last thing I want to do after what Noel did to me. I thought I'd never forgive him for putting me in this hole, but I have to admit things are improving.

Actually, I rather like the daily ward routine and being left alone for most of the time. I've started writing again, mostly poems. Every day after Group we have what they call Practical English with Mr Pettigrew. All the other adults around here are happy to be called by their first names, but he's not. I suppose it's the teacher in him. Behind his back we call him Pettypants. I don't think he'd approve. His face is red and shiny, with pouchy jowls. He tries to get us to 'engage with the page' as he calls it, but no one except for Holden and I is interested in schoolwork. Pettypants genuinely tries to help me with my studies: he phones my school and gets in some textbooks my class is working on, as well as some novels for English. And when I worry aloud about getting behind in my school work and maybe having to repeat this final

92

year, he takes time to try and reassure me, which is kind of him.

Today, my brain fuzzed with reading chapter after chapter of *To Kill a Mockingbird*, I stare out of the window and daydream about Matt. The others pretend to work. Not Lauren and Ashley, though. They sit and gossip or flick through glossy mags. Pettypants tries to quieten them.

'Ladies,' he says, 'please put those magazines away and keep your chatter down. Others are trying to work.'

Lauren swears at him, loudly.

Pettypants sounds as though he's choking. 'I beg your pardon?'

'You heard me, dickhead.'

There's a long silence.

I glance up and see that Lauren and Ashley are staring brazenly at him, but he's taken an easy option: he's walking away. Just as well, too. They would have torn him up. I feel sorry for him; it can't be easy having students coming and going all the time and not having any continuity with us.

I'm beginning to know a bit about the others here, even though I keep my distance from them. Emma walks around as if spaced out. I think it's more than being off her face on meds: at meal times the nurses try to encourage her to eat, but she barely touches her food. She's twig-thin so maybe she's anorexic. I was friends once with a girl who had anorexia. Jessie. She wouldn't listen to anyone who told her she needed to put on weight. She insisted she was fat. Jessie used to invite me over to her place and we'd give one another beauty treatments – facials, hairdos and manicures. She had this big collection of teddy bears. When she was really sick and I went to visit her in hospital, she gave me her favourite. Just after that, she died. I still have her bear – always will. Cuddly One sits on my bed at home with Mopsie, my politically incorrect golliwog, which Arlene knitted for me when I was little. I suppose it's childish for someone my age to have such things, but we all need something to love.

Holden has this compulsion about numbers. He counts tiles on the floor, lines on the ceiling, lights in the ward – not once or twice, but over and over again. Another guy, Felix, admits in Group to having panic attacks. You can hear the terror in his voice when he talks about being alone or getting lost. 'When it happens,' he says, 'I can't breathe. I get nauseous. I sweat. My heart races – it feels like I'm going to die.'

I feel sorry for him; we all do, I think, except Lauren.

'You're a loser, Felix.' She smirks. 'And a wanker.'

Ashley giggles at that. She and Lauren are best buddies. They get off on putting everyone down. I thought I liked Lauren, but now I'm not so sure.

Matt's written to me three or four times now. And he forwarded a letter from Greta. It's full of news from school and what everyone's been up to. All light and fluffy stuff. But at the end there's a serious bit:

I'm sorry I walked out on you at the pub that night. Fact is I couldn't handle it when I saw you'd been cutting yourself. I'd made up my mind that people who did it were crazy. But you're not crazy. I think you're more sane than I am. I've been reading lots about cutting – there's stacks on the net – and I've realised I was being really judgemental. So please forgive me for being a shitty friend. I am trying really hard to understand. And who am I to judge? I've had a cushy life and I've got a great family. You don't seem to have anyone. I care about you, Sophie. I can't wait for you to get back to school so we can hang together.

Greta's signed off with heaps of hearts and kisses and hugs. And she's drawn all these silly little cartoon figures. Sooo Greta. Her letter is special. It lifts me higher than any drug they've fed me in this place.

Amy hasn't written at all, the slacker, but that's Amy. She means well, I'm sure, but she never gets around to doing stuff. Matt writes that college classes and assignments are taking up a lot of his time, that he's working long hours at the market (which is why he hasn't visited again) and – most importantly – that he still misses me. I don't reply to the letters. I'd like to, but does anyone really want a girl in a loony bin pouring her heart out to them? I get so intense sometimes and it comes across in my writing. They'd be sure to get a twenty-page letter, plus my soppy poems. I'd freak them out. No, I'll catch up when I get back home.

Home. Just saying the word evokes all kinds of feelings in me. I want so much to resume a normal life – or as normal as I can ever have. Seeing Matt and Amy, Greta, the gang from school . . .

I think about that all the time. But it scares me, too. More and more as I stay in this shut-off world with its daily routines and safe walls, I find myself burrowing in. It has become my refuge, my hiding place. I know when the time comes it will be hard to adjust to the 'real' world, to home. I'm not really sure if I can do it.

In therapy today, Helen started by reading to me from the Department case file Marie must have given her. I heard Marie's clipped tones in the writing, so impersonal on such a personal subject. When Helen mentioned the Pattersons, a forgotten anger surged in me.

'Those bastards,' I muttered.

Helen looked at me, almost surprised that I had a voice, let alone such an angry one. I'd managed to avoid words before this. Ordinarily I would have dropped my head, but today I couldn't turn away. She smiled at me. Pale blue eyes, sharp and intelligent. There's a dimple at the right corner of her lip.

'It's very nice to hear from you.'

I nodded.

'Such a relief,' she said, 'I was beginning to think

I'd only ever see the top of your head.'

I like her smile. In fact, I've decided I like her. She laughs a lot. You can hear her in the corridor a long way off. Other doctors and staff tiptoe around patients, and mostly talk in subdued tones. But Helen is upfront, noisy and colourful in this soulless place. I still don't feel like talking to her, though. So many people have claimed a piece of me over the years that I have come to mistrust everyone, except Matt. Even he hurt me when he met Greta at the pub, although maybe it wasn't as bad as I imagined at the time.

After Group today Lauren fronts up to me. 'You want a smoke?' she says.

There are *No Smoking* signs all over the hospital but they don't mean anything to Lauren. She lights up and glares when I don't want to do the same.

'Sorry.' I smile. 'I'd join you if I smoked. But I don't.'

Lauren considers me intently for a moment. 'I thought you were a stuck-up bitch when you first got here, but maybe I was wrong. Still workin' on that one.'

I say nothing, but glance sideways and see that on the inside of her arm are scars, raised and pink, bright ugly worms of things. She sees me looking but doesn't comment.

'What are you in here for?'

'Homicide,' I answer, very grimly.

Her eyes chase down the truth, burning into mine.

Finally I smirk.

'I knew it! You're full of bull!'

We both laugh then. It's the first time I've laughed in weeks.

It's a rare sound from patients in a place like this – unless it's some manic giggle. A nurse at her desk peers at us curiously. Lauren turns her back to hide the cigarette.

'Nosy bitch,' she mutters. 'You can't fart in this joint without someone writing a report about it.'

That makes me laugh again. Lauren can be nasty but right now she's good medicine for me.

'Tell us about that guy who came to visit you.' She leans in closer. 'He's hot.'

'Oh, Matt,' I casually reply. 'He lives with me.' It feels so good to say that. Of course, I don't mention we're only flatmates.

'Yeah? Far out. Tell me about him.'

'Sorry, it's private.'

She glares. For a second I think she's going to hit me. But then . . .

'I suppose I can understand that. If I had him I'd be just the same – half your luck.'

That night I doze off holding the idea of Matt close to me.

14

*A*t first I sat dumbly in Helen's office, but now I've started – tentatively – to react to her questions. She asks me this morning if I'm feeling happier. 'You were laughing with Lauren in the Day Room when I came in,' she says.

'Lauren can be funny sometimes.'

She is taken aback to hear a reply, but doesn't comment, so I continue. 'But I guess none of us here are really happy, no matter how much we pretend, or we wouldn't be here.'

She smiles, her lips like a crescent moon laid on its side. The smile is in her eyes, too. As much as I want to keep my distance, it's difficult to ignore the growing feeling that she cares about me. Unlike Noel, she has told me a lot about herself in those earlier sessions. And she has demanded nothing from me.

'Would you like to tell me what you know about your early childhood?' she asks.

The kindness in her voice cuts through my defences.

I tell her what I remember. How I never knew my father, how first there was just me and my mother.

'She was skinny, I think. For years I had a purple fluffy teddy. I seem to recall that she gave it to me. One of my carers' dogs tore it to pieces. I cried for days after. That's about it . . .'

'Nothing more?' she says, the faint curve of a smile at the corners of her mouth.

'Well . . . one day my mother took an overdose and I rang the emergency services. So they tell me. I don't remember it.'

'That was brave of you.'

'Not really.'

'Do you remember anything at all about that night?'

I try hard for her.

'Um . . . being scared of the cops.'

She waits patiently. No pressure.

'I'm pretty sure there was a fat woman who cuddled me and took me to her home. She gave me an ice-cream and sang to me when I went to bed.'

Helen looks so peaceful.

'I can't remember anything else.'

'You did very well. I think that's enough for today.'

I'm amazed that the session has come to an end so quickly.

'I wanted to ask something.' I hesitate. If she says 'no' to me I'll feel so hurt. From anyone else it

100

wouldn't matter, but from her . . .

'What is it, Sophie?'

That kindness again − it gives me the strength I need.

'Ever since I've been here I've been stuck in the ward. Can I go out? Into the grounds?'

'I don't see any problem with that. Of course.'

'I can go with my friends?'

'Yes. I think that's a very good idea.'

I feel she's drawing me closer to her with everything she says, with every look. My Helen.

Later that afternoon a group of us is allowed outdoors. The hospital is set in vast grounds, with whole areas of grass stretching green and unbroken for a long way. There's a tarred driveway leading up to the entrance gates about half a kilometre away, so, for something to do, we dawdle together towards it.

We're a strange lot. Holden counts to himself as he walks − his lips moving − so many steps this way, so many that way. Someone is always asking him about it, and every time, head down he answers, 'I have to'. Poor guy. Meanwhile, Felix keeps turning to glance at the hospital as if to reassure himself it hasn't vanished since he last looked. And Ashley, who acts like the Roadrunner on speed, has dashed ahead and is calling for us to, 'Hurry up! Hurry up!'

Lauren ambles along beside me, her eyes fixed on the gates ahead. They are chained but not drawn tightly together. She soon confirms what I'm thinking.

'If someone pushes it open for me, I reckon I can squeeze through there.'

Ashley overhears her. 'It's only fifteen minutes walk into town. You want to do it?'

'Yeah!' Lauren charges at the gate. 'Let's all go! Come on!'

Felix and Holden hang back.

Holden shakes his head, not at all keen on a break-out.

Briefly, Felix considers it, before deciding that the opening is too small.

'I might get stuck,' he says.

'Fine!' Lauren snaps. 'I didn't want you freaks anyway.' She looks at me. 'But you're comin' – right?'

There's no way I can. Helen trusted me, trusted all of us.

'Don't do it,' I say. 'It's not worth it.'

With Ashley's help, Lauren wiggles through the opening. 'Wrong!' she yells back at me. 'You're not worth it! You're a loser, just like them! Come on, Ashley – move it!'

She strains against the gates so that Ashley can squeeze through. And then both of them are on the other side. 'Let's go!'

Without a backward glance, Lauren and Ashley stride down the tree-lined road towards town.

Holden, Felix and I return to the hospital not saying a word to one another. Hours later the three of us are called in to the head sister's office. I refuse to say anything, but Felix tells her what happened. Later, I see Helen and rush up to her.

'I'm sorry – about Lauren and Ashley: I tried to stop them.'

'I know you did,' she says. 'It's not your fault, Sophie. You did nothing wrong.'

She is so forgiving, how could I not help but feel happy?

Just before lunch the next day, Ashley is brought in. She shuffles like a zombie between two orderlies, staring ahead, as though a doctor has given her a massive dose of drugs. Or maybe she's taken something herself and is tripping out. They put her into a private room and lock the door.

Lauren doesn't return the following day, or the next. It is four days before she troops in, cheeks bruised, bottom lip swollen and bleeding. She catches me watching her as she's escorted along the corridor.

She screams, 'What are you looking at, bitch?'

For hours afterwards I have a lonely, empty feeling in my gut. Once, for half a minute, I thought we could be friends.

Today, for the first time, Helen is late for our session. I keep checking the wall clock in the nurses' station as the minutes tick past our appointed time, but she doesn't show. She's always punctual. I stop a passing nurse.

'Where's Helen?'

'Probably caught up somewhere.'

'She's never late.'

'She'll be here.' As if the nurse cares.

Ten, twenty, thirty minutes pass. I begin to feel panicky, my heart drumming at a berserk tempo.

At long last Helen strides along the corridor towards me. 'Sophie,' she calls, panting. 'There was an emergency. I'm so sorry to have kept you waiting.' She fumbles for the keys to her office door while I stand mute, unable to form a sentence. There's a pain in me, as though a rib is cracked.

In her room, Helen tosses her keys onto the desk and turns toward me, a smile breaking across her face. My throat feels full of cut glass, tears swim across my eyes.

Through the blur, I see Helen's face, pasted over with a mild look of confusion, her mouth open in surprise.

'Sophie, what's wrong?'

'I thought you weren't coming.' Even as I half-say, half-sob this, I feel like a stupid two-year-old.

'Oh, you poor thing.' Before I know it, she has her arms around me, pulling me towards her soft, spongy chest. My heart turns liquid with need. When did I ever cry so much in all my life? Hurts that have been trapped for so long cascade out in tears onto her jacket front.

Finally I'm reduced to hiccups, and then to silence. We stand, embracing one another, with Helen gently patting my back. I hold her closer and closer until there's not much world left. A feeling of peace overcomes me, a sense of being perfectly content, as if I have tuned into some great harmony and am in a place I was always meant to be. Never have I felt like this. Before I was fragmented: now Helen has put all the pieces together.

Afterward we sit opposite one another as we always do and there are her questions, my answers. Something is different. Ballooning inside of me is a feeling I can only describe as love. It's nothing like the affection I have for Matt. This is more intense. Dangerous.

15

*S*ince the session this morning with Helen, my pen has been racing, trying to capture the momentous emotions I'm experiencing. I feel so creative, so alive, so energetic. I love Helen. I thought that would be hard to say, but it's not. I truly love her. And now I want so much to offer something to her that will go beyond the walls of her office, something that she can take with her when she leaves here at night. I am going to create a poem for her.

I write, then scratch out, write again. It is tortuously slow to form. All my words seem inadequate. I want to say thank you for so many things: for being real with me; for not hiding behind platitudes; for allowing me to be so vulnerable; but mostly for holding me, in her arms, like a mother.

'What are you writing?' One of the orderlies, a big guy, looms over me.

I slam shut my book and clutch it to my chest. 'Nothing,' I mumble, not daring to look at him.

'Really? You seem to be very busy writing nothing.' He chuckles to himself as he goes on his way.

There's no privacy here, no peace. I don't have a locked door to hide behind. But I do have my journal. I look at what I've written. Ever since I can remember, I've experienced intense, momentary yearnings for older women – school teachers, mostly, but even women in the street. I imagine being held by them. The idea of sex with a woman doesn't interest me, so I don't think I'm a lesbian. I just want the closeness a woman's embrace – a motherly embrace – can give me. I daydream about Helen, trying to recapture the intense feeling I experienced when she held me, trying to imagine her hand stroking my face.

Late at night, unable to sleep, I sit in the waiting room off the nurses' office and finish my poem for Helen.

In the Beginning
The sun has dropped from the sky,
You peer into the girl's uplifted eyes,
Her mind ingrained with belief:
'Love cannot abide here,
it is a stranger.'
Her tongue is wood, and, you suspect,
Her heart.
Undaunted,
You reach out,
Think
If only this were enough,

The opening of hands
To help unload grief,
Heal the soul that has not yet
Learned love.

Endless mother, physician,
You begin to undo the tongue
Like bandages,
Release memories
Too powerful to escape from

Like stars being born,
Sparks begin to rise into air.

Slowly, slowly,
The dark is melting.

I'm happy with the poem. More than that, I think it's the best I've ever written. If it is good, I owe it to the deep feelings that Helen has awakened in me. But I'm anxious about showing it to her. What if she doesn't like it? Or just skims through it? Or gives me a polite smile? A platitude? I'll be crushed.

When the meds are handed out after dinner, I pretend to swallow mine. I want to have a clear head in the morning when I give Helen the poem. I lay awake most of the night thinking about her, going over every scenario, too scared for sleep.

Next morning when it's my therapy session, Helen smiles and gestures for me to sit. I place the poem on her desk.

'Is this for me?'

'Yes.'

She puts down her pen and takes my poem in her hands. I love the way she reads it in silence, slowly, thoughtfully.

My heart pounds when finally she looks at me.

'You write beautifully, Sophie.'

I feel like crying.

When it's time to begin talking today, words burst from me.

'Arlene and Dutch were my aunt and uncle who cared for me when the Department took me from my mother,' I say. 'She was into drugs. Used to steal so she could afford her habit. I was too young to re-member, but Arlene told me that the reason she and Dutch took me was because of neglect. Apparently my mother would just leave me, sometimes for days at a time. I didn't see her much after that. When I was about four or five, she vanished altogether.'

Helen's eyebrows rise.

'Vanished?'

'I don't know where she went. Who cares? Maybe she overdosed and died in an alley somewhere. Stupid junkie.'

She doesn't comment on that or criticise – she never would – but I feel I have to explain because I know I must seem hard.

'She was never like a real mother to me, Helen, not the way Arlene was. She and Dutch were so good

109

to me. They tucked me into bed at night, read stories or sang me to sleep. I could always go to either of them if I had a problem. I loved them.'

'Did they have other children?'

'No, just me. And they treated me like I was their own.'

Helen smiles in her gentle way and my mind drifts . . .

I remember the day I started school. The moment I saw the other kids I wrenched my hand free of Arlene and rushed away to join them in a game. When I thought to look up, I was amazed to see her crying, her shoulders heaving as if something dreadful had happened. It affected me to know, even back when I was so little, that someone really did love me.

The same feelings sweep back now. Helen passes me a tissue. I touch her hand as I take it.

'Are you okay, Sophie?'

'Yes.' *As long as you're with me.* 'I'm fine.'

For the rest of that day, I withdraw into the whiteboard room and scribble down a multitude of memories which talking with Helen has ignited.

I remember Arlene sending me to birthday parties, always in the prettiest frock, with the biggest and best gift. When I joined the Brownies, Arlene attended all my badge presentations. She taught me the alphabet, how to read, how to tie my laces, how to swim, to sew, to knit, to bake a butter cake. She and Dutch were both proud of me. They boasted to their friends whenever they had the chance. About me.

There are other memories, too. I try to shut them out, but I can't. Sometimes, when Dutch had too much to drink, he'd tease Arlene until she grew tetchy and snapped at him. Sometimes I lay in bed and heard their loud voices, and shivered with fear. I never thought that either one would hurt me; it was more that I had lived with that fighting and shouting when I was with my mother. She had left me, and in my heart I suspected it was all happening again.

The next day I read to Helen what I'd written.

'*Arlene and Dutch were waiting for me one day when I came home from school. There was a visitor, a stranger who turned out to be Marie. "We've something to tell you, sweetheart," Arlene said.*'

I pause, gathering myself together. It's harder than I thought it would be to share, even with Helen.

I read on.

'*Their faces looked so serious; Arlene's eyes were red-rimmed. I stood there, confused, unable to speak. They were getting a divorce. Arlene had a new boyfriend and they were going to live interstate. Dutch was taking the next flight home to the Netherlands. There was no place for me.*'

'That's a very sad story,' Helen says when I pause. 'How did it make you feel to read it to me?'

I look away from her, holding in my feelings. She gives me a few seconds before continuing.

'What happened next?'

'I pleaded with them to change their minds. It was a big shock to me, you know. I thought I would be

111

with them forever.'

Tears are dribbling down my cheeks; my bottom lip quivers.

'Go on,' encourages Helen.

Marie says, "I'll be your caseworker. You'll go to live with a foster family while we try to find your mother." I put my hands on my ears; I didn't want to hear her. I begged Arlene, I begged Dutch. I went from one to the other saying, "Please, please, please. Don't. I love you. You're my mummy and daddy.".'

I pause, wiping my eyes with the back of my hand. 'I was so pathetic.'

'No you weren't,' Helen murmurs.

'Arlene was crying, and I said, "Can't I come with you?" She said I couldn't. She never said why. Dutch wouldn't even look at me.'

'That must have been so hard.'

'I couldn't understand how they could just erase me like that, as if I had never existed, as if I had meant nothing to them. It made me feel worthless then, and it still does now.'

'No, don't say that. You're not . . .'

'I was only a child, and they threw me away, like I was a piece of rubbish!'

'Sophie . . .'

Helen holds out her hand and I take it. I never want to let go.

Memories of Arlene and Dutch haunt me for days after. When they finally leave it's only because I crowd my mind with images of Helen. She becomes my first waking thought and my last. During the day I hang around the nurses' station hoping someone will say something about her. Or I sit outside the entrance of the ward where I can see staff cars approaching down the driveway. When I glimpse Helen's car I scuttle indoors so she won't see me. I don't want her to know that I watch out for her. When feelings are as intense as mine, people back away. I don't want that to happen to us.

My sessions with Helen have changed from how they used to be. Now the doors are wide open, the walls of secrecy have tumbled to the ground. I want Helen to know me. Not the shell of a person I usually let people see, but the real me. Memories that have been locked away come flooding back, some good, some bad, but with Helen guiding me, I can handle anything. I talk about thoughts and feelings and hopes: yes, I have hopes now.

One day Helen wears a beret to work. It teases out a memory of a hat that my mother wore. She used to pull the brim forward to partly cover her face, so that when she grabbed someone's handbag, they wouldn't recognise her. Helen and I look across the desk at each other. She has a bemused penny-for-your-thoughts look. It occurs to me how wonderful it would be if she was my mother.

'Can you remember anything else, Sophie? About your early childhood?'

'Yes. My mother used to make me wait in places while she went off: she never told me what she was doing. I was always scared that she wouldn't come back.'

Helen soaks up every word as if she is actually back there with me, waiting in some lonely street.

'We lived in an abandoned car for a while ... Have we got time for this, Helen? Am I talking too much?'

'No. Never. Please go on.'

'Okay. We lived on the street in a car. It was bad: people banging on the doors, tapping on the windows. Now, when I get in a car, first thing I do is slam down the locks. And there was this motel we stayed in sometimes. A real dump: wallpaper peeling, a terrible smell. All through the night we'd hear arguments, swearing and yelling, doors slamming. It was such a hell of a place.'

I let the air rush out of me with a great sigh.

Helen leans forward to rest a hand on mine.

'You're doing well, Sophie. It's brave of you to talk about these things.'

My eyes are closed. I concentrate on the touch of her hand, drink deep from the sound of her voice.

16

*F*inally I hear from Amy. We're not really allowed to take phone calls (nor are we allowed to have our mobiles) but I've only had Matt come to visit me those few times, so maybe the nurse feels sorry for me when Amy rings.

'When are you getting out of that place?' is her opening question.

'Who knows?'

'Are they, like, doing strange things to your brain?'

It's at that very moment I realise why Amy probably hasn't contacted me before now. Her mother. Her poor demented mother who walked out on her. Who abandoned her. The thought of Helen screwing with my brain, attaching electrodes or drugging me to get at the truth seems so absurd. If only Amy knew how I spill my guts freely, how I look forward to doing it.

'No, nobody's messing with my head. I promise, Amy.'

She peppers me with questions and I duck and

weave my way through them.

'Okay. Enough about me,' I say. 'Tell me about the real world.'

'Thought you'd never ask! I've got these new piercings. In my navel and one in my right nipple. So sexy! And a great tatt on my butt. You ought to see them!'

I laugh. 'I'd rather not, thanks all the same.'

'You're jealous, Soph – I know. When you get out of there you should get yourself some tatts. I'll take you – hold your hand if you like.'

'No, I've told you before, I'm not interested and I don't know why you would be.'

She protests. 'I'm making myself a work of art. It's about improvement. Like I'm claiming my body for my own. You can understand that, can't you?'

I pause, bite my lip. 'Yes. Yeah, I guess so.'

We chatter on some more before I bring up the subject that's most important to me.

'How's Matt? Is he coming to see me soon?'

There's a hesitation at the other end and I have a sudden fear that Amy's going to tell me Matt has taken up with a girl and hasn't got time for me. But it's not that.

'He's okay,' she says at last. 'He had a prang on his bike.'

'Oh no! Is he all right?'

'Geez, cool it, will ya? He's fine. He busted his hand, that's all. It's only a little break.'

'Thank god it wasn't serious.'

'Nah. He's tough. Only thing is, he's not supposed to drive for a while. That's why he hasn't been in to see you. He's going to write to you, so you'll hear all about it – all the gory details.'

'I'll write to him, too,' I say. 'Will you tell him that I . . . tell him that I hope he gets better soon? And make him look after himself!'

'I've already done that,' Amy says. 'I told him, next time you fall off your bike, make sure you land on your head – nothing important to hurt that way.'

We end the conversation there, both of us laughing.

So my life continues at the hospital and I go on sharing my feelings with Helen. Each time that I dredge up a memory, another is there waiting in line for its chance to be heard.

As I sit across from Helen I'm flooded with emotions. She thinks I cry because of the stories I tell her, the broken promises and the sadness. But the real reason is that I can't say how I truly feel, about her. How much I want her to hold me again. But then if she did, I'd need to ask for more; I'd beg for it. There is no limit to my need. I want Helen to stroke my face, to tell me she cares about me, that she loves me. I want to become her child.

My heart clenches when each session with her ends. I want to scream, to say that she can't go, I won't let her go. The only thing that stops me is that I know she will be back the next day, and the next. When I leave her office, I find a place of my own, close my eyes and relive the session. I see Helen so clearly. She is beautiful.

Sometimes, as a way of holding her with me in the long hours when we are separated, I try to sketch her. And always I write in my journal about all the hopes I have for us. More and more, she is my family. I don't even mind that she has a daughter: she can be my sister. Helen has enough love for both of us. I try to imagine her home and picture myself in it, sitting with Helen or being held by her.

> *I want to touch the edges of her face,*
> *soft and smooth as Mother Love.*
> *Contained within her*
> *is a whole continent of understanding.*
> *Unwinding a coil in my heart*
> *she has become*
> *the one blade of grass*
> *in a never-ending desert.*

'What are you writing all the time?' It's Ashley's turn at interrogation.

'Nothing important.'

'I bet you're writing about being in this place and all about us, huh? Is it going to be for a story or something?'

I've learnt how to handle Ashley. Be aggressive

118

with her and you'll get it back twice over. Much easier to go along with her.

'You guessed it,' I say. 'It's a movie script about this place.'

'Bull . . . Really?'

'Yep. It's true.'

'Yeah, right.' She considers this for a moment, before adding, 'I better be in it.'

'For sure,' I lie.

To my dismay she pulls up a chair for herself.

'You see Marshall today?'

That makes me angry. It's Helen! I want to say. Helen! But then it occurs to me that they don't share a special relationship, that's why she doesn't use her Christian name. My anger quickly dissipates.

'Yes, I'm seeing her.'

'Me too. What do you talk about?'

'The usual things.'

'I tell her all sorts of stuff. Really sick stuff.'

I hate her saying these things to me.

'She probably gets off on hearing it.'

'She does not!' I'm on my feet and standing over her.

'What's up with you?'

I grab my book and start walking.

'Nothing,' I call back. 'Just stay away from me.'

Soon I'm sitting opposite Helen again.

'Today I think we should talk about your suicidal feelings,' Helen says.

She's dressed as usual in a suit, dark blue, with a white blouse. Her hair is looped into a knot at the back of her neck but strands have come loose and hang in wisps around her face. Her skin is pink and well-scrubbed. She doesn't wear make-up. I notice for the first time that there's a small scar on her forehead.

'Sophie . . .'

'Yes. Sorry. What were you saying?'

'Why don't you tell me about what happened the last time you tried to kill yourself?'

'You know about that?'

She nods. 'Doctor Palmer spoke to me on the phone.'

Noel. He keeps stepping into my life, trying to sabotage me.

I take a deep breath and try to focus but I can't.

'You took some sleeping pills,' Helen reminds me.

'Yes.'

'Perhaps you can tell me what happened. Where did you get the pills?'

'Do we have to talk about this? It's all finished with. Can't we just leave it dead?'

'But is it, Sophie? Is it really dead?'

I stare out of the window.

'We need to talk about what keeps making you want to harm yourself.'

I won't do it again now I have something to live for. I've got you, Helen.

It kills me that I can't tell her that simple truth.

I sigh. 'They were Shirley's pills.'

'I don't think you've spoken about Shirley before . . .'

'Shirley and Doug Patterson. My last foster parents.'

'I see. And can you tell me what led up to your taking them?'

Tears well in my eyes and cascade down my cheeks. Helen hands me a tissue and I tear more from the box. There never seems to be enough tissues for me nowadays.

'What can I tell you?' I say hopelessly. 'They weren't bad people. They weren't child molesters. But they didn't really care about me. I was worth so much a month to them from the Department, that's all. And I was lonely, Helen. Desperately. I only wish I could have found more pills.'

'Do you feel alone very often?'

I'm all emotion, incapable of even one intelligible sentence. Sobbing and sobbing. All the years of feeling that no one on this earth gives a damn about me are tumbling about inside of me – exploding.

Helen doesn't try to stop me from crying.

My world brightens when Matt comes to visit again. It feels like forever since I last saw him but really it's only been a couple of weeks. He's brought me a silly teddy bear with a bow tie.

'It shouldn't have a bow tie,' I tell him.

'Why not?'

'Bow ties are a guy thing. And the bear is pink . . .'

'Well, not everything is perfect.' Matt holds my hand as we walk across the lawn, spied on, I'm aware, by half the kids in my ward.

'We're being watched,' I say.

He shrugs. 'Forget about them. The important thing is, what are we going to call our new bear?'

'*Our* bear? I thought you gave it to me.'

'I did, but it's a share bear.'

I smile. 'Then that's its name. Share Bear.'

We sit with our backs against a tree, as far away from prying eyes as possible.

'How are things with you, Soph?'

'Terrific!'

'Really?'

'Don't I look better?'

'Well, you do seem happier. Are you?'

'I am, Matt, for the first time in so long.'

Helen is the reason for the happiness, but it might hurt his feelings if I share that with him.

'Greta's rung a few times,' he says.

'Oh . . . you and she been seeing much of each other?'

'No. Why would we?'

'That night at the pub. Remember? Your eyes almost fell out of your head.'

Matt's face reddens. 'Aw, that was nothing. She asks about you. Greta is not interested in me, I promise.'

'But are you interested in her?'

'No. Not a bit. You know, Soph, I don't go around giving bears to just anyone.'

I'm flattered, I'm knocked out. Here's this sweet guy saying beautiful things to me. Sheltered by the tree, we huddle close. I have Helen. And Matt. In this moment, I can't imagine being happier.

17

The day has come that I've feared. I'm to return home, back to the cottage in Collins Street with Amy and Matt. Back to school. Back to therapy sessions with Noel.

'You're out of your depression now, Sophie,' Helen says. 'You're no longer a danger to yourself.'

'But . . .'

'Yes?'

'But what about us? Won't I see you again?' Suddenly I'm blubbering, feeling about two years old, barely articulate.

'You'll miss me?'

I shake my head wildly. 'No! No!' 'Miss' doesn't even *begin* to describe how I feel.

Helen turns her head slightly to one side, her way of inviting me to explain.

I force myself to say it. The hardest thing I'll ever say.

'I love you.'

A wisp of hair has caught at the corner of her

mouth. She closes her eyes for a moment, then sighs, long and deep.

Whatever she says now doesn't matter. I won't ever take back what I said. It's there for all time. I love her. I just love her.

'What you're feeling, Sophie,' Helen says, 'is not love. It's called transference. It's common for patients to have feelings of transference for their doctors. They transfer feelings they have for other people onto their therapist.'

'Please will you hug me again?'

She shakes her head. 'I can't, sweetie, really I can't.'

'But you did before.'

I'm engulfed by wave upon wave of the most devastating pain imaginable.

Helen's face is a mask. After pausing a moment, as if weighing up her options, she says, 'I'll prescribe some medication. It'll calm you.'

'No, no! I don't want tablets! There's nothing wrong with me! Can't you understand, Helen? I just love you!'

The look she has for me changes. The gentle love I knew before is gone. Her eyes are full of pity.

It all becomes a blur then. At some point I take the prescribed tablets. They numb me, but the pain of rejection feels like it is going to consume me.

I want to cut myself. And cut and cut. Erase every skerrick of the agony. I can't imagine going home or returning to school or anything else. If I can't see Helen again, I don't want to live.

The final session. I go in there determined to keep my self-respect, to hold my head up. But in the end, pride doesn't matter.

'You'll soon be back with your friends.' Helen smiles. 'I know you'll be happy there.'

'But I like it here. It's peaceful. Can't I stay? I won't be any trouble. I can work outside in the gardens or help you in the office. I'll clean if you like. You just tell me what to do, Helen, anything at all and I'll do it. But please don't send me away.'

'It's human to want something good to last forever.' Now Helen sounds so stiff and formal, as if her heart has turned to stone. 'But everything inevitably changes.'

'I don't want to leave you.'

'You can't stay here forever, Sophie. You need to get back to your life. To the outside world.'

'If I leave, can I keep on seeing you?'

Helen shakes her head briskly. 'I want you to continue your therapy sessions with Doctor Palmer. I'll send him a report on your progress, and I want you to be as honest with him as you have been with me. Okay?'

'I don't want to talk to Noel,' I sob. 'It's you I want to talk to, Helen, you, not him. I love you.'

'Now, Sophie . . .'

'Please hold me.'

'No.'

'Please,' I persist. 'Just once more. Then I'll never ask again.'

'You must go.'

The words stab into my heart. *You must go.* There is nothing more that Helen offers. She starts tapping into her laptop as if I have already vanished. All the hurt in my life is nothing compared to this cold dead moment.

Marie comes to collect me. I can't bear to talk to her, to look at her. I'm in turmoil; old desires are new again and festering inside me.

At the ward front door I walk past Lauren and Ashley. They speak but their words don't sink in. Holden, Felix and Emma are nearby. I recognise the word 'goodbye', but I ignore them.

All I want is to see Helen, and I can never do that again.

In the car, Marie fires questions at me. How could she begin to understand? How could I ever trust her?

I look out of the window through tears and say nothing.

Amy and Matt are at the house when we arrive.

'I'll be okay now,' I mutter to Marie as I get out of the car. She shrugs and drives away.

There is a handmade *WELCOME HOME* sign strung along the length of one wall. Emotion bubbles up when I see it and then they both hug me. It feels good.

Amy has shaved her head and is tanned and healthy. Matt is the same as always, tall and good looking, his eyes warm and friendly.

I feel awkward at first, but my flatmates treat me as they always do. They are both full of smiles and happy chatter but despite their efforts, all I want is to escape to my room. I can't though, not yet. I go along with their hospitality as we sit around the table over mugs of coffee and look at one another.

'Well,' I say, trying to sound cheerful, 'here we are again.'

'About time you came back,' Amy says. 'Matt's becoming lazy. I need you to help me boss him about.'

'*I'm* lazy?' Matt gapes at Amy. 'You should talk.' He turns to me. 'I've had to do all the work since you left, Sophie. Ames here hasn't lifted a finger!'

That of course spurs Amy into action and insults fly back and forth, none of them serious. At another time I might have enjoyed their pretend battle. Not now. My head and my heart are back at the hospital. I'm sitting opposite Helen or she's hugging me, yes, she's hugging me, her warmth enveloping me. I'm safe in her arms.

Matt touches my shoulder. 'Hey, Soph. Good to have you back.'

'Yeah,' says Amy. 'It really is.'

I smile but feel weak and distant. I can't fake being happy right now.

We sip our drinks and Amy tells me about her new boyfriend, Johnny. 'We're going on a holiday tomorrow. Up the coast on his motorbike, camping out.' She runs her fingers over her spiky skull.

'And I did my exams a while back,' Matt says. 'I did pretty good. Much better than I expected. Had some time off work because of my hand and I was actually able to study for once . . .'

I can't take it any longer.

'I'm really tired.' I stand abruptly and head out of the room. 'I have to go to bed.'

In the dark, my eyes closed, Helen holds me. 'I love you, too, Sophie,' she says.

Sleep is impossible. I miss her so much. Keep saying her name. Can't stop. Don't want to. Helen. Helen. Helen. It is a physical pain I feel – in my chest, my head. There's only one way to be rid of it. I find the razor. I am carving Helen's initials on my arm. I am bleeding for Helen. I stand at the mirror. 'See, Helen. This is how much I love you. I will never stop loving you.'

Only when my arm is cut and streaming with blood, when the pain from the cutting soars above the pain I feel for Helen, only then can I sleep.

18

*N*ext morning I meet Amy's Johnny, a tall, bulky guy with tatts, and farewell the two of them on their trip up the coast. Then Matt and I are left together. He tries to initiate conversation. In a stumbling, hesitant way he touches my arm. I move away from him, shut him out. Finally he leaves for his job and I'm alone. I water Amy's pot plants, remembering how Helen told me that before the latest rainfall she'd had to buy in a tank of water. Then I wash a few dishes, thinking how hard it must be to live in the country. I turn on the television and sit petting Amy's cat, Persia. He purrs and I wonder if Helen has a cat. Or perhaps she has a dog. She's so loving I'm sure she'd have some kind of pet.

The TV's on but I'm not watching. I have my own show playing, in my mind. Helen. I know that her middle initial is M. What does it stand for? Mary? Margaret? There can't be many Helen M Marshalls. I flick through the phone book. There are four with that name. Only one suburb looks right for her, the others are too far from the hospital. I think of the mud I saw on her tyres every morning it rained. It has to be rural; it has to be Eagleton Valley.

I feed Persia, put him outside, get my sweater and leave the house.

I'm out on the street and the sky is black with rain. I hardly feel it. I'm walking towards Helen. Just that thought has sewn me back together, all the jagged pieces of me slip into place. This is how it was meant to be. When she turned me away before, it was a test. Anyone can say, 'I love you'. It's too easy. It only has true meaning when you back your words up with actions. I understand that now. You'll see, Helen, you'll see. No one will ever love you as much as I do. We were meant to be together.

It's early afternoon by the time I get out on the highway. The rain drones on, hard and cold. I put my thumb up and stand at the edge of the road, so close to the cars I could lean out and touch them as they flash past. I've never hitched before but it doesn't worry me. I'm not scared of anything now. I clutch Helen's address in my hand and feel like I have a little piece of her with me, protecting me.

Finally a car pulls over.

'Better get you inside out of the rain, luv.'

It's a woman in her sixties. Her face is gaunt, not at all like Helen's.

'Thank you.'

'You know, a young girl like you shouldn't be hitching a ride – it's not safe these days.'

'It's an emergency.' The lie comes so easily. 'I have to get to Eagleton Valley. A friend is sick.'

'Eagleton?' She thinks about it for a few seconds. 'Yes, I know where that is. I can get you close to there.'

I don't reply. Not even when she smiles at me.

I'm going to Helen.

At the end of a steep driveway set into the side of a hill, I peer over a metal fence. Helen's house is not as grand as I'd imagined; it's ordinary. Wooden, with a corrugated iron roof. The view across the valley, though, is beautiful. There's an orchard in front of the house, and beyond that, rolling green hills.

I feel compelled to explore further, but now, suddenly, I'm nervous. Helen ought to be at the hospital at this time of the day, but she might come home for a late lunch. I want so much to see her again, but I couldn't stand it if she turned me away. In time she'll accept me into her life, I know she will, but I have to be patient. For now I'm happy just to have seen where she lives. When I dream about her, I'll be able to see her in this little home set on the hill. I'll see her car puttering down the dirt road and turning into her driveway and I'll be there to greet her. She'll get out of the car and she'll hold me again. Like Arlene once did. Like my mother. This will be my home, too.

I walk back to the highway and hold out my thumb to the approaching traffic. I feel so calm.

I had left the hospital with the idea of not being co-operative with Noel but after having gone to Helen's home, Noel doesn't bother me now. Nothing does. I feel like a child with an enormous secret that she's bursting to share.

'Welcome back, Sophie. It's good to see you again.'

All I can do is grin with happiness.

'You seem more cheerful today than I've seen you in the past.'

I feel like giggling but restrain myself.

'You seem so happy, Sophie. Would you like to tell me about it?'

'What's to tell? I'm happy. So? That's a good thing, right?'

'Yes.' He rubs his chin, perplexed. 'Of course.'

I throw it back at him.

'Are you happy?'

'Yes, thank you . . . How was your stay in hospital?'

'It was okay.'

'Hmm . . . You saw a doctor while you were there?'

He's opened the door and I am more than glad to walk right in. 'Helen Marshall. Her name is Helen Marshall. She . . .'

I feed him little morsels about Helen, about how I care about her, only I don't use the word 'love'. I

133

don't want to share that with anyone but her. Noel sits, as always, fingers interlaced, intently listening to me, occasionally murmuring, but never commenting, not letting me into any part of his world, not the way my Helen did. When I have talked for a long time, he smiles at me, a smile I have never learned to interpret. We sit in silence as he waits for me to continue, but I've said enough. I close my eyes and listen to the clock ticking. A few moments later his voice intrudes.

'So you have strong feelings for Doctor Marshall?'

'Not really. I just like her.'

'I see.'

He doesn't really. He never will. That part of my life is not for anyone else to see.

Noel looks at the clock and says, as he always does at the end of the session, 'I'm afraid we've finished for today, Sophie. But we'll talk more next time.'

I leave him, my secret safe and warm inside me.

The rest of the day seems long and loose. I gaze at the bloody initials on my arm, and trace my finger around the letters HM. It draws me even closer to her.

When Matt finally arrives home, it's good to sit with him. If he wonders why I run so hot and cold he doesn't comment. With a beer to keep us company, we discuss movies, music, and our pet hates, before the conversation winds around to this: 'Do you want to talk about being in hospital, Soph?'

'It wasn't too bad. I survived.'

'Thought you might have been scared.'

'Of what?'

'I don't know – the other patients?'

'No way. They were scared of me.'

'That I understand.'

I see his cheeky smile.

I tell him a few anecdotes about the other patients, careful to avoid any cheap joke about loonies that might get an easy laugh. That tends to happen when you find out you're one of the loonies yourself. And I do drop Helen's name, making it seem almost an afterthought.

'Oh, and there was this woman I met who was nice. Helen. She was my doctor.'

'Did she help you?'

'Yes. Yes, she really did.'

Just the mention of her name, even so casually, has an effect on me. I have to change the subject.

'Anyway, that's enough hospital talk,' I say. 'What have we got to eat?'

'There's hardly any food in the house,' Matt says. 'Tell you what – let's go shopping. We'll stock up on groceries and later I'll cook dinner for you. Sound okay?'

'Sounds brilliant.'

We snack on chips in the car on the way to the shops. In between bites we share our favourite eating experiences. It's a game Matt likes playing. Name the food and the place you had it. And explain why it is memorable.

'Hokey-pokey ice-cream,' Matt says. 'White chocolate ice-cream laced with honeycomb pieces. I had it when I was on holiday with my family in New Zealand. I was ten. It was the best thing I'd ever tasted – but I dropped it! I cried like I never have, before or since, and my mum bought me another one. I went from abject sadness to absolute bliss. Unforgettable. Your turn, Soph.'

It's not hard to choose. It will have to be something I ate when I was living with Arlene and Dutch, because the other times I don't want to remember.

'*Poffertjes,*' I say.

As expected, Matt replies, 'Huh?'

'It's about the only Dutch word I know. They're mini pancakes. A big favourite with people from Holland. A sprinkle of sugar, some butter. Yum! I used to have them when I was with my aunt and uncle. I'll make you some one day.'

'You've got a deal,' he says.

I like the idea of sharing things with him. One day in the future. When you've been passed around between as many families as I have, you crave any sense of permanency in a friendship. Later, as we stroll around the supermarket filling our trolley with groceries, thoughts of Matt jostle with deeper thoughts of Helen. Matt hangs close, as if we're a couple and a part of me yearns for that to be true. But I can't stop thinking of Helen.

She wraps her arms around me and I snuggle my head against her chest. I'm at such peace.

'Soph – Sophie.'

Matt holds up an avocado. 'Does this look ripe enough to you?'

I squeeze it and nod.

He crosses it off his list and goes back to perusing the fruit and vegetables. I go back to Helen.

When does she do her shopping? Weekly? Daily? Do we buy the same sort of breakfast cereal? The same washing detergent? I want to find out everything about her; what she eats and drinks, the clothes she wears when she's not at the hospital. Is there a man in her life? She looks so beautiful there could easily be one. But my heart tells me there isn't. She's alone. She needs someone to look after her . . .

'Hey, Sophie.'

Matt is smiling at me.

'You seem so far away. You okay?'

'Perfect,' I say. 'Everything is perfect.'

At home, Matt lines up all the ingredients he needs to make dinner. But first there's a question: 'Anyone you'd like to invite, Soph?'

I play with the idea of inviting Helen, but I know that's impossible – for now at least. I'm about to say no when I have a sudden idea.

'Yes, there is someone, Greta. That all right?'

'Sure. No problem.' Matt doesn't hesitate. 'We eat at seven. How about you crash between now and then – you look really tired.'

No arguments from me. I fall onto my bed, but before I let myself doze off, I ring Greta. I want to be overwhelmed by her cheeriness. I've missed it. I'd also like to see for myself if there's any chemistry between her and Matt.

'Sophie!' She is her usual bright and bubbly self. 'How you been?'

'Home from hospital. All fixed up and better than new.'

'Fan-bloody-tastic!'

Her unbridled enthusiasm blasts down the phone line and puts a smile on my face. I love that about her. And of course she's as mad as a rabid hatter, so we have much in common.

'Would you like to come to dinner tonight? Matt's cooking.'

'Cool. I'm in.'

I start to give her the details, but don't get very far.

'Hey listen. Before I come over I want to set you straight on something. I know you were upset that night at the pub because you thought I was coming on to Matt.'

'No I wasn't, Greta. What are you talking about?'

'Yeah, well, I might have got it wrong. But just

so you know, there's nothing going on between us. Never was. I was just mucking around flirting with him, wasn't ever interested in him, really. I've already got a guy. His name is Reece. Wait until you meet him. He's a hunk. Anyway, Matt's already taken – by you.'

'Greta, you're insane.'

'Open your eyes, Sophie. Every time I rang to ask after you, all he could do was rave about how wonderful you are. I was getting really annoyed.'

'You're such a liar.'

'Dead set, the guy likes you heaps.'

'I don't believe a word of it,' I say, but secretly, I do. Greta continues to chat. Soon the words form one continuous blurred line. In contrast, in vivid sharpness, is Helen's face. I was really happy to hear what Greta said about Matt, but now that feeling passes. I can't concentrate on anything else but Helen.

I make my excuses and get off the phone. Sleep comes fast. It is deep and peaceful because I don't feel alone.

The dinner party is excellent. Greta is wild and witty and dominates most of the conversation. Matt is the perfect host, even if the food is overcooked. Doesn't matter one little bit. The only disappointment is me. No one comments about it, but I feel and act like sludge. I just cannot lift myself into a happy state. My insides feel prickly and restless. Questions are treated to one word answers. Twice I catch myself snapping at Matt – for no apparent reason. More and more I retreat into a cocoon.

'Sorry,' I say. 'I have to take stupid medication. It makes me exhausted. And bad company.'

They both try to cheer me up.

Matt says, 'You're doing fine, Soph.'

'And you're always great company,' adds Greta.

Such liars. Such good friends.

Around midnight I announce, 'I'm off to bed, before I fall asleep at the table.'

Matt and Greta party on, her voice and laughter ringing through the house high above his. I've stopped feeling jealous of her now. She's much prettier than I am but she's not really Matt's type. He's quiet, like me.

I bury my head under a pillow to shut out all sound, but though I was exhausted when I came to bed, now I can't sleep. Moments with Helen come back to me. I linger in them, never want them to leave. It's been forty-eight hours since I last saw her but tonight she stays with me, every minute.

When I wake in the morning, groggy yet strangely energised, I know I have to go to the hospital to visit Helen. I can't stand another day without seeing her. She needs to know how I feel about her. If I showed her how I cut her initials into me, then she'd have some idea. But I won't have to go that far. I'll just walk

140

in there and her eyes will light up. 'Sophie!' She'll throw her arms around me and it'll be like I never went away. I know she didn't mean for us to never see each other again. Helen isn't just any doctor. She can't be judged by the same rules as others. The feelings that we share are unique. I know what happened between us. I know the love that she gave me. I know I don't ever have to be scared with her.

Within a short time I head out to catch the train to Marstown, the hospital's closest station. The suburbs rattle past in a blur. Pretty soon I am walking down the long driveway and then I'm in the foyer near Helen's office.

'Sophie.' It's one of the psych nurses who was on duty when I was in hospital. 'What are you doing here?'

'I need to see Helen.'

'Oh. Okay. But you can't see her without an appointment. In any case, she's not here today.'

I feel alarmed. 'Is she sick?'

'No.' She looks concerned. 'Can someone else help you?'

I smile as though I haven't got a single care. It's the best way to stop her from getting nosy.

'It wasn't important.'

A patient comes up, demanding the nurse's attention, and I slip away as quickly as I can.

Back at the hospital entrance I sit under a tree,

wondering what to do. I've come such a long way without seeing her, and now my feelings are more intense than ever. I feel so close to Helen, yet so far away. I need her terribly.

19

*T*he shadows of trees are lengthening and it's almost dark as I climb the last hill. It's been a five kay walk and for every step Helen has been beside me. Hands shoved deep in my pockets for warmth, I visualise her coming to her front door. The look on her face when she sees me – that will be the moment that decides everything. Once she gets past the surprise, will she be happy or sad? No, not sad. Why would she be? I'm a friend. I hope, of course, that she'll wrap her arms around me. I've imagined that so many times. Perhaps, though, it will just be a handshake at first; her strong hand cupped in mine. 'Welcome, Sophie,' she'll say. 'Welcome.'

The closer I get, the more frantically my heart beats. This is almost too much to take. It's terrifying. It's sublime.

With the moon just beginning to rise, I walk down her driveway, gravel crunching underfoot. At the front of the house is a wide veranda. I mount the wooden stairs to the door, pause, and then knock loudly. Boldly.

No one answers. Mist hangs in the air and a sudden coldness rushes through me. I rub the tops of my arms as I look out over the valley. The trees are bare-limbed in the orchard, and far away down the hill I can make out the faint shape of another house. It's so isolated here.

As I walk the perimeter of Helen's house, I see a sedan with an interstate number plate parked in the side carport. Nearby is a barbecue area stacked neatly with wood. Did she cut and stack the wood herself? Who owns the car? So much to explore. So many questions. Further along, I look through a window into the laundry.

Back at the front of the house, I climb the stairs again and put my face up close to the glass in a window. A dining room leads into a lounge room and further off to the right through a doorway is what might be a bedroom. Perhaps it's hers . . .

I jiggle the front door handle. To my utter surprise, the door opens. Why has she left it open like this? I wonder as I step inside Helen's house. I'm scared but elated at the same time. It's as if I'm tripping on a drug that no one knows about but me. And it feels so much as though I belong here. For a while I stand stock-still, listening to my breathing, aware of my heart thumping. The moon is shining into the lounge room. In the corner there's an opened roll-top desk with Helen's briefcase on it. I'm tempted to pull out the patient files to see what she's written about me, but I know that wouldn't be fair to her. I never want to hurt her, not in any way.

On the wall of what I'm sure is Helen's bedroom is a corkboard covered with photographs. There's one of her when she is much younger and thinner, looking pretty and proudly holding up a baby for the camera. I wonder where her husband is. There are a few photos of her and an older couple who I take to be her parents, and other photos of her with couples who could be siblings. But there's not one that indicates a partner. She needs someone in her life to look after her. I've always thought that, and now I know for sure. I put my finger to a photo and stroke her face. At that moment, it feels like we're the only two people in the world . . .

I find a recent photo of her. She's smiling with those small, perfect teeth, her sense of humour obvious. I have to have it. She surely won't notice it's gone, and it will bring me comfort when I'm missing her.

I'm freezing by now, having left home without warm clothing. There's a jumper draped over a chair so I pull it on. Immediately I'm enveloped by Helen's warm, musky aroma. Eyes closed, I feel the delicious sensation of being whole and loved and secure. On a small table is a bottle of moisturiser. I rub some on my hands, inhale the scent. Then I pull back the patchwork cover on the bed and lie under it. When I was little I would put on Arlene's high heels and lipstick and call myself a princess. Now I am better than a princess. I am Helen, alone in my sanctuary, no patients to worry about, relaxing and enjoying the serenity of this moment. 'It is so good to have you visit, Sophie,' I say to the young woman I love. 'You are welcome to stay here for as long as you like.' She spreads her arms and welcomes me into her embrace.

As I lie here, blissing out, I'm startled by a flash of light cutting across the room. A car is in the driveway. Helen! I jump out of bed, pull off her jumper, and run onto the veranda, closing the door quietly behind me, and then leap to the ground where I disappear behind some bushes. There I crouch low, listening. I hear a car door slam, then another, the sound of voices – Helen, and her daughter, Cara. Wooden stairs creak under their weight as they climb. The door opens. They talk to one another, but their words are indistinct. I squeeze into a space under the house, moving closer to the voices until I'm directly under where they are talking.

'It's been a long day for both of us. As soon as you brush your teeth, it's off to bed, darling.'

'Can't I stay up just a bit longer, Mum?'

'I'm afraid not. School tomorrow.'

'But Muumm.'

'Cara . . .'

In the silence Helen is hugging her. I know because I can feel it. I hold myself tight, wishing her arms were around me. I decide to stay here where I am close to her, at least for a while. Sitting with my back against a brick foundation, I listen: murmurs and footsteps, the flushing of a toilet, the clicking of switches. Then all is still. Helen is safe in her bed and I wish I was there beside her. I feel her, soft like a fluffy pillow against my skinny frame. I so want to be close to her, to be held by her. Like a child with her mother. Without her I feel so empty.

For a long time I consider knocking on her door again. In a few minutes I could be inside, sitting next to her on the lounge. She'd see that I was cold and wrap a rug around my shoulders. I can hear her loving voice so clearly, 'Sophie, my dear . . .'

I am almost sure that's how it would be, but I have to be cautious. I can't take the risk of being turned away. There is nothing that could be worse than that.

Coldness intensifies as the night draws on. I'm shivering, and I don't like the idea of walking along that country road alone. No, it's better to stay here and endure the cold. I settle myself as best I can, folding into a curled shape for warmth, and close my eyes. A moment later I'm wrenched into wakefulness by something landing on my face. A spider. I gasp and slap at it. So much noise. I listen in the darkness, fearful that Helen or Cara might have heard me but nothing stirs. Soon I give myself to sleep, whispering Helen's name, over and over.

All through the night I'm cold and restless, constantly startled awake by a rustle that could be a rat, or a feeling of repulsion as the memory of the spider looms large. I sleep again only to wake confused and frightened – *what am I doing in this damp, alien place?* My one redeeming thought is the knowledge that Helen is near. With that in mind I drift back to sleep.

Eventually morning comes. A rooster crows on a nearby farm. Footsteps in the house. A cat comes to examine this dishevelled stranger. It's ginger and white and arches its tail, rubbing itself against me and purring. I stroke it. 'I'm Sophie,' I murmur, 'Mummy's friend.' From the back door, Cara calls 'Puss, puss,' and the cat, running, leaves me. A radio blares: news, weather reports, music – all the morning things – toilets and showers, toast, coffee. Helen and Cara are talking, their voices muted. Soon doors slam. A car engine starts up. Moving across to a trellis near the back door, I peer through it and see Helen in her car, turning to reverse up the driveway. I want so much to run out to her calling, 'Helen, Helen. It's me – Sophie! Please stay home with me today.' Courage fails me though and I remain transfixed until the car is at the end of the driveway and I can no longer see my dear Helen.

20

As I'd expected, Matt's at home, waiting anxiously for me.

'I'm starving,' I reply to his quizzical expression.

'I don't want to hassle you, Soph,' he says, 'but I was worried about you.'

'I'm sorry; I couldn't get to a phone.'

'You could have phoned, if you'd really wanted to.'

His insistence annoys me. 'The truth is I couldn't.'

'You couldn't get to a phone? Not one? Couldn't borrow a mobile?'

'I don't owe it to you to tell you every little thing that goes on in my life.'

'I've got a right,' Matt insists.

'What right?'

Matt's face is flushed but he meets my gaze, challenging. His voice is skating on the thin edge of anger. 'Damn it, Sophie, you've just come out of hospital, and I thought . . .'

I move to stand in front of him. 'What did you think?'

'That maybe you'd hurt yourself.'

'Don't be stupid.'

'Don't call me stupid!' Matt's face is transformed.

'Well you are stupid, if you think you own me!'

'Stuff you, Sophie! Why do I bother with you?'

'I wish you'd stop! I wish you'd just get out of my life!'

He looks at me strangely. It feels like we've hit the borderline. We're right on the edge of goodbye, and yet he hangs back as if he's reluctant to take that final step.

'If that's what you want.' There's no anger left in his voice. His eyes lose the lion that was in them only moments ago.

I turn my back on him. Arms folded. Spikes in my heart. I want to run, to escape from this house. But where would I go? This is all I have. And yet home doesn't seem to fit anymore. I feel like a husk, a snail shell without its snail.

'Sophie?'

Now I face him, the silence between us like a black hole. Words are caught behind the fence of my teeth.

'It's all too much,' I finally reply. 'I don't want you putting any pressure on me. I can't take it.'

Matt sighs. 'Is it pressure, Sophie? I thought I was just showing you that I care – isn't that a natural thing to do when someone means a lot to you?'

I'm touched by what he says, but I'm not ready to

show it. Maybe I'm scared that it's not real.

'I'm not used to people caring,' I say. It comes out stone cold.

Despite this, he moves towards me, ever so slightly, as though he wants to hold me. And I want to hug him close to me, so tightly that we become one. I can't, though. It's another borderline. One I'm not ready to cross. Not now.

'I'm sorry,' I mutter, turning for my room.

On my bed I imagine I can hear Arlene's voice, soft as smoke, whispering comforting words in my ear, anchoring me with love. I so much want her and Dutch with me again. I take out Arlene's old nightie and hold it against my cheek trying to rekindle a memory, a time when I was at peace.

I drift into my past. I am seven years old, pig-tailed and sprawled on the living room floor making a library of my books, writing a card for each one, gluing stars against titles, depending on how much I'd enjoyed reading them. Dutch is in his armchair, a glass of beer beside him, listening to the horse races on the radio. Arlene is sitting at the dining table, straight-backed and neat, writing a letter. I am looking up at these two people I love so dearly. All is right with the world.

Holding onto this vision I pass into a deep and dreamless sleep.

———

That afternoon I have another session with Noel.

'Hi!' I say, brightly.

He nods and his smile broadens. 'You look cheerful today.'

'Maybe I had a great time last night.' It's so tempting to tell him. 'Maybe it was incredible.'

'And did you have a great night?'

Helen's in my head. She's sleeping and I'm under her house again, almost as if I'm guarding her from harm.

Sweet dreams, Helen. No one will hurt you while I'm here.

'I might have.'

'Are you going to tell me?'

I can't help grinning. 'No – but you can guess, if you like.'

He shrugs, a smile still lingering.

What's she doing now? Having morning tea? Has she noticed that photo missing? The one that's in my pocket at this moment?

'Is there anything you'd like to talk about, Sophie?'

'That depends. Are you sure it'll be confidential?'

'Well . . .'

Noel launches into a speech about how most things are confidential, but if I confessed to a crime, like murder, he'd have certain legal obligations.

'Have you broken the law?' he concludes.

'Don't think so.'

'Mm,' he murmurs after a long silence. 'Perhaps you'd like to share it with me.'

I do want to tell him about Helen. To say her name aloud, not to hide her away in my mind, but I think back to the last time I spoke openly to Noel: he betrayed me and I ended up in hospital.

'No. I've got nothing to share with you. Not a thing.'

He nods, ever patient. I've played so many mind games with him and this is simply another. 'I respect your decision, Sophie.' He leans back in his chair, awaiting my next move.

I tiptoe inside Helen's house, into her bedroom. She looks so perfect. Her flowing hair hangs loose around the pillow, framing her face. I tuck her in gently, struggling to control my breathing — it's so loud and frantic — but I do. And then I breathe in time with Helen, rhythmic and peaceful.

'Sophie. Sophie.'

I wriggle back into reality. Time has passed so quickly. Noel glances at the clock. The session's coming to an end.

'I'll see you next week.' He stands at the door. 'Perhaps you'll share your secret with me then.'

'I might.'

For now though, Helen's safe in my heart.

At home I lie on my bed, eyes closed. Helen is swimming in the ocean. It feels as though I'm high above, watching from a cloud. I think about swimming laps, how it helps me move out of the tumult in my head. Side by side, I would love to swim with Helen, stroking through the water, looking across at her and smiling! That thought puts me in a serene mood.

By the time Matt gets home, it feels like a cloud has lifted. 'I'm making dinner tonight,' I say. 'You have two choices: spaghetti or spaghetti.'

'Gee,' he says, 'that's a tough one . . . I think I'll have spaghetti.'

I've missed this, I decide, as I potter around in the kitchen. Cooking, being active – it helps me get out of my head. And it's great to be able to do something for Matt for a change. He's been so good to me.

'Enjoy!'

'Thanks, Soph.' He twirls spaghetti around his fork. 'I'm so hungry.'

My thoughts fly back to Helen. Are she and Cara having dinner now?

'Sophie.'

'Yes?'

'You didn't answer – I was talking to you.'

'Oh sorry, Matt. I didn't mean to be rude. What were you saying?'

'I've become friends with the new neighbours. You haven't met them, have you?'

'No, I haven't.'

'There's a single mum, Joanne, and she's got four kids.'

'Wow.'

'Yeah. They're nice kids, but what a handful. They moved in a few weeks ago and since then . . .'

I drift away again. Can't help it. More to the point, I don't want to stop.

I wonder if I should write to Helen. She told me I'm good with words. Was she inviting me to write? It's a perfect way to be close to her again, and she couldn't possibly mind it. A poem. Yes. I can say so much in a subtle way with poetry. Tell her how much I miss her, how much I want to see her again.

Soon I'm conscious of Matt standing, collecting the dishes. He's hardly touched his spaghetti.

'Was everything okay?' I ask.

'It was fine,' he says. 'I just wish you could have been here to enjoy it with me.'

'I don't understand, Matt.'

'You didn't listen to a thing I said.'

'Yes I did. The new neighbour – she has four kids.'

'Sophie, I said lots more than that. You disappear into your dream world all the time. You've never been this bad before. What's up with you?'

'Nothing.'

'Okay. Forget it then. Forget it.'

He stands at the sink with his back to me. I walk over and put my arms around his waist, locking my hands in front of him.

'There is something going on, Matt. And I do want to tell you about it . . . but I don't think you'd understand.'

'Yes I would. No matter what you said, I'd understand.'

'I can't tell you. Not yet. Give me time. Please, Matt.'

His hands take mine and clench them tight.

'Okay, Soph. Take all the time you need.'

I make a conscious decision not to let thoughts of Helen intrude for the rest of the night. It's selfish of me. Besides, there'll be plenty of time for that when I'm alone. For now I have to stay focused. On my suggestion we're going to visit our new neighbour. I've raided the cupboards for goodies and come up with an assortment of biscuits and chocolates for her kids. For Joanne I pick some daffodils that Amy has grown – I know she won't mind. I wrap them in red paper and tie a ribbon around them.

'What do you think?' I ask Matt.

His glorious smile says it all.

Joanne opens the door, her blonde hair standing on end as though she's had an electric shock.

'Hello. It's Matt from next door.'

'And Sophie.'

'Oh, hello,' she says. 'This is a surprise.'

I hand her the gifts. 'These are from both of us. We wanted to welcome you.'

'Really?'

'I didn't have much to do with it, to be honest.' Matt looks at me. 'Sophie did it all.'

'Aw. That's so nice of you. Now come inside – please – meet my family.'

Three small boys in PJs come rushing towards us.

'Who are you?' demands the youngest. He's freckle-faced and has two front teeth missing.

'I'm Sophie.' I smile down at him and he grins back.

'This is Sammy,' Joanne says.

'Are you Matt's girlfriend?'

I can feel myself blushing as I shake my head, but this doesn't stop him. 'Mattie's got a girlfriend, Mattie's got a girlfriend!' he chants at the top of his voice as he hurtles back down the hall.

The other two little boys are watching me and laughing.

'Don't mind Sammy,' says Joanne. 'You'll get used to him. Say hello to Sophie, Mike. You too, Ricky.'

'Hello,' they chorus.

The lounge room, as we pass through it, looks like a tornado has struck. In the kitchen, a girl of about thirteen is washing up. She looks a bit like Cara. 'This is my lovely Olivia.' Joanne holds her close.

Olivia turns to me, a smile peeping out from

behind shyness. 'Hello.' She has a pretty face but you have to look past the pimples and crooked teeth to appreciate it.

'Leave the dishes, sweetie.' Joanne taps her lightly on the back. 'You have a talk to Sophie and Matt while I make us a cuppa.' Turning to Matt and me, she asks, 'Coffee be all right?'

Olivia is sweet, and she's intelligent, too. She tells us about school – 'I think I'll be a scientist when I grow up' – and pulls a face when I ask what's it like to have three little brothers.

'They're very smelly,' she says, oh-so-seriously, as if describing a scientific experiment. 'But they're all right, I suppose – for boys.'

All too quickly I ease myself out of the conversation. I hear Olivia chatting and Matt asking her questions, but the words stop having any meaning . . . I'm writing a letter.

Today I met this young family. I'm sure you'd love them, Helen. There's this girl who's so much like Cara. It must be great to have a daughter. What sort of things do you do together?

'Here you go, Sophie.' Joanne has a cup of coffee in her hand. 'Do you want sugar?'

'No thanks.'

Matt frowns at me. Focus, I tell myself. Focus.

As we talk, Sammy, Mike and Ricky dart in and out from the lounge room where they're supposed to be watching TV.

'Mum! Mum! Ricky punched me!'

'Sammy changed the channel!'

'Mum! Mike spilled his drink on the carpet!'

'I'm thirsty!'

'I'm hungry!'

Every five seconds brings a major drama. Joanne answers each call without complaint. Nothing is too much trouble. Olivia helps, too, fetching water, rocking one of her brothers on her knee. In many ways she's more like Joanne's younger sister than her daughter. It could be like that with me and Helen. I might be able to help her in the hospital; filing, typing – any number of things. I'd sit with her in the car each morning and go home at night to dinner and a fire. Spending every day with Helen would be incredible.

'You okay there?' Joanne has her hand on my arm.

'Sure. I'm fine.'

'Sophie's been taking some medication,' Matt says. 'For headaches. Right, Soph?'

'Yes.' I smile. 'It's doing all sorts of funny things to my head. I find it hard to concentrate.'

'It's not serious is it, the problem?'

'No. Nothing a new head wouldn't fix.'

'I could do with one of those, too.'

Joanne's face crinkles as she laughs. I like her, and her kids, too, especially Olivia. We chat some more and the conversation twists and turns until she's telling us about her new part-time job.

'I'm doing some bar work down at the club,' she says. 'I love it but it means that I have to leave Olivia in charge of the kids at night – only for a few hours though.'

Call it my maternal instinct, or just plain stupidity. Whatever the reason, I eagerly volunteer to help.

'Hey, Joanne,' I say, 'anytime you need a babysitter, here I am – and I work for free.'

'Do you mean it?'

'Of course I do.'

'I won't ask unless I really have to – maybe if I get stuck with a long shift one night.'

'It's not a problem. I'd love to do it.'

'That's so generous of you, Sophie.'

Joanne hugs me. She almost feels like Helen.

Before long the boys have become so noisy and demanding that Joanne announces it's their bedtime.

Back at home, Matt says, 'That was nice of you. Saying you'd babysit the kids.'

'Just something to do,' I reply, shrugging it off.

'You know, Sophie –' He takes a step forward. 'One of the qualities I like most is kindness. You've got heaps of it.'

It seems a perfect time to kiss him, if only I didn't feel so conflicted. If one day we do kiss, I want to mean it with all my heart.

'Thanks,' I say, and leave it at that.

'Well then . . . Goodnight, Soph.'

'Night.'

In my room I take out Helen's photo and trace my finger around the shape of her face. 'Goodnight, my dear friend.'

21

*B*efore heading off to see Noel, I do something I haven't done for ages: I take myself for a long walk through town to the beach. It's a gorgeous early spring day, the air crisp, the sun shining and a slight breeze ruffling the seaside grasses. I lie in my shorts and top on the sand and soak up the ambience. It's so good being without a care, revelling in the sun on my face and body, breathing deep, smelling the tangy aroma of salt air.

At last it feels as if things are starting to come together. I'm settled at home with Matt and Amy. Just thinking *home* is very special. And I liked meeting the neighbours. I hope I'll see more of them. Best of all, I feel closer to Helen. Now I know where she lives I don't feel so lost and alone. It's as if I have a get-out-of-jail card in my back pocket. If things ever get really bad, I can see her. And I know that as soon as she puts her arms around me, I'll be complete.

All morning I've been trying to write a poem, a gift for Helen. I want it to be something she'll cherish. Now I'm watching surfers, wondering if Helen ever swims here at this beach, and letting my mind grasp at images for the poem. I sit scribbling furiously for a long while. Gradually words and phrases glide into place. Until at last it's finished.

All the way to Noel's office I debate whether or not to show him the poem. Will I? Won't I? I'm like a very small girl with a very big secret. We're only five minutes into the session when I mention I've written it. 'For Doctor Marshall.'

'A poem?' He curls the word around as he says it. 'How interesting. And why did you write it?'

I shrug.

'Would you like to show it to me?'

Still unsure, I find myself nodding anyway, and I pass it across the desk.

'Shall I read it aloud?'

'If you want to.'

On sun-soaked weekends
the sea drowns it —
the anguished confessions,
other people's pain,
that might become hers
if she did not dive beneath the long green claw
that curls above her,
plunging through water that goes
forever down.

In her swirling, buoyant element,

her mind unlocked,
she hears
the watery world singing around her,
deep-throated
and pregnant with freedom.

Noel's gaze lifts slowly from the page, and falls on me.

'Well, well. You have a gift with words, Sophie.'

'No big deal.' I'm ecstatic that my writing has impressed him.

He takes another look at it, nodding as he reads.

'Yes. This shows a great deal of empathy and compassion.'

'Thanks.'

I want to snatch the poem back now. He's read it. I've got my praise. Let's move on before he starts examining every word for hidden meanings.

'You seem to understand that Doctor Marshall needs to have a life apart from her patients.'

I say nothing. It's safer that way.

'You're going to post it?'

I've already decided I'm giving it to Helen in person, but I'm not telling him that.

'Probably. I'm not sure.'

'How do you think she'll feel, reading your poem?'

I shrug at first and then add, 'I hope she likes it, of course. Nothing strange about wanting that, is there?'

'Not at all. It's a perfectly natural thing to hope for.'

Now I do take the poem back. Folding it carefully before placing it in my blouse pocket I say, 'Finished with that. New subject.'

'What would you like to talk about today?'

'You tell me, Noel.'

He raises an eyebrow. So atypical; he hardly ever does anything that lets me know that he has had some kind of emotional reaction to what I've said.

'What?' I ask.

'*Noel?* You've never used my Christian name before.'

'You don't want me to?'

'I don't mind. I was just wondering, why today?'

'That's how I think of you.'

'Since when?'

'Since forever. Though I did give you a nickname when I first met you . . .' I pause, waiting for his response.

'Is that so?'

'Yep.'

'Are you going to tell me?' he says after a while.

I grin. 'Have a guess.'

'I have no idea.'

'Go on . . .'

'I wouldn't know where to start.'

'Freudie Babe, that's what I called you!'

'And why is that?'

'Well, you're a shrink . . .'

'Yes?'

'And you look a bit like the photos you see of Freud.'

Noel ducks his head and smiles broadly. I think it's the first time I've ever seen him smile so happily. He seems kind of cute, like a benevolent father.

'Can I ask you something personal?'

Noel purses his mouth, says nothing. I take the plunge. 'Do you have a family? Are you someone's dad?'

'Why do you need to know about my family?'

'God! Now we're back to this "you make a statement and I repeat it or I ask a question" game. I just wish for once that you would give me a bit of power in this relationship. Or that we could be equals – for even a minute!'

He puts up a passive-face shield. Impossible to know what he's thinking. It's championship chess.

After a while I break into the silence by saying, almost flippantly, that I miss the hospital.

'Oh?'

'Well, not the hospital exactly. Things about being there.'

'Doctor Marshall?'

The poem told him everything, so I might as well spit it out. 'I want to see her again.'

'And why is that, Sophie?'

I stare at the photo on the wall of the boy and girl

166

kissing and say nothing more. What is there to say? It's obvious he doesn't approve. There's bound to be some law against it, some stupid rule. But he can't stop me. No one can.

'Perhaps we can talk about this next time,' he says.

It's time to go again. My life is a procession of clocks and doors. I'm only of interest for a certain amount of time. After that doors are only opened to let me out, to be rid of me.

Noel smiles. 'I liked your poem, Sophie.' And he closes the door.

22

$\mathscr{M}$arie comes to visit. She brings with her a pile of school work which teachers have sent to be finished over the holidays. I look at the work – including three thick novels to be read – and moan.

'There goes my two weeks of fun!' I complain.

'I'm sure you'll still find time for fun,' Marie says. I expect her to scuttle away as she usually does but this time she sits down and isn't in a hurry.

'Perhaps we could have a cup of tea together,' she suggests, 'and a little chat.'

I can manage having tea with her but the chat sounds ominous. This woman doesn't spend time with the likes of me unless she has to. Soon we're sitting opposite each other, drowning in a sea of awkward silence. And then the bombshell drops.

'We've been thinking, Sophie, that it might be a good idea for you to go back into fostering.'

I stare at her, dumbfounded, and shake my head. The urge to cut jerks into my mind.

'We've been discussing your case . . .'

It's not my case, it's my life!

'And there are very real concerns about your well-being, especially if you're having suicidal thoughts.'

'I'm not! Who told you that? That was weeks and weeks ago. I'm all right now. Helen – the doctor at the hospital – has given me antidepressants, and besides I've promised her if I get depressed again I'll talk to Noel about it. Doctor Palmer.'

'Yes, well that may be so –' Marie's attempt at a smile makes her look like she has a mouthful of prunes – 'but as you can appreciate, we are charged with your care. It would be remiss of the Department not to act if we had any doubts about how you're coping.'

I try to stay calm. Try to think Helen into my mind. She won't come. Too much panic.

'I can't believe this!' I bang my head down on the table. It hurts but I don't care.

'Now, now, Sophie, it's this very sort of behaviour which makes us concerned. You are a risk to yourself, dear.'

'I'm not! I'm happy here. I like being with Matt and Amy. We get on really well.'

'But they aren't always here. Are they? Hmm? Now we have in mind a really nice couple who've fostered teenagers for years . . .'

Helen. Helen. Helen.

'I'd like to take you to visit them. I'm sure you'll be very happy there.'

'I won't go.'

'This is in your own best interest.'

I take a deep breath, regroup. Yelling and banging my head is only going to give her more ammunition. I have to be calm in this storm, as Helen would.

'I've learned coping mechanisms from Hel – from Doctor Marshall at the hospital.' I speak quietly and slowly. Back in control now. 'And I'm working with Doctor Palmer. If you move me again now, when I'm at last settling down, you would do so much damage, Miss Jarmine. That's the only reason I'd hurt myself. Please don't make me go.'

I can almost hear the wheels of thought tumbling around in Marie's mind. And as she drains the last of her tea, I can guess what she's thinking. *If we do force this on her, and she does kill herself, then it could come back and implicate us at the Department.*

'Well then,' she says, placing the cup on the table, 'this is something that will have to be considered. I'll take this information back to my supervisor and we'll see what we can do. I'd like to report that you're feeling better. Is that the case?'

'Much better.'

'And you're still seeing Doctor Palmer twice a week?'

'Three times.'

'Excellent.'

'And he's helping.'

'I'm so pleased. Now I want you to think about

that placement I mentioned, but for the time being, since you seem to be making progress, we might just keep things as they are – but of course, my supervisor will have the final word.'

When Marie has gone, I sit for a while, trying to overcome the compulsion to cut. Talking to Helen in my head helps. I know she'd be disappointed if I cut myself. I close my eyes and picture her holding me. 'Be calm,' she keeps repeating. 'They won't move you again. You're safe where you are. Safe with me.'

Before long though, I'm in the bathroom, the razor in my hand. I can't keep doing this but I have such need. I look in the mirror and find Helen's face. No, I won't cut myself, I tell her. *But I need you so much.* In my head, ever so faintly, I hear her calling, *Come to me.*

I put the razor away and grab a jacket. I'm going to see my Helen at the hospital. I'll give her my poem. The thought of being with her again restores my spirits.

Outside the train window there is sunshine and children playing and bright colours. The world is alive and so am I, the need to cut fading with every passing station, with every step I move closer to Helen.

However, at the hospital there is a brick wall.

'I'm sorry.' The secretary cleans her glasses as

she speaks. 'You can't see Doctor Marshall without an appointment. In any case she's booked up with patients all day.'

I'm disappointed of course, but not shattered. Secretaries always think they know everything. They know nothing.

'That's okay,' I reply. 'No problem.'

I take a seat in the waiting room, find a good magazine, and settle in. Helen always comes to the door to say goodbye when she finishes with a patient. The next time her door opens, I'll be there. The secretary rolls her eyes when she sees me still there, but she doesn't say anything.

The clock ticks slowly and loudly. Just before the hour, a bundle of bones comes in and sits opposite me. Anorexic, and a patient for sure. Does Helen show her the love that she showed to me? The thought of this girl being hugged is unbearable. I glare at her, blatantly, rudely. She burrows her gaze into a magazine, not daring to look at me. 'Why can't you just go away?' I say it so loudly the secretary looks up. I glare at her, too.

Twenty-seven minutes pass, and then a man with dreadlocks and a scruffy beard walks out of Helen's consulting room. I see her. And she sees me.

'Sophie!'

I want to rush into her arms but my legs are stuck in cement. My brain is calling the shots.

Let there be a sign from her first. Let her say my name

again, not in shock but affection. Wait.

Helen looks perplexed. 'We don't have an appointment, do we?'

'No. But I need to see you.' I mumble, embarrassed that her patients are staring at me.

Helen gestures for me to follow her. 'Come into my office for a moment.'

Yes! I knew she'd see me. I knew it!

But then, before the door is even closed behind us, she changes – her tone, her features – all have suddenly grown cold.

'You are Doctor Palmer's patient now. I thought I made that clear. You can't just turn up, Sophie. It's not acceptable.'

I'm crying. Unable to stop. Unable to stand. I lie on the floor. I want to sink into it and disappear.

'Up you get.' Helen's strong hands help lift me to my feet. 'This is childish. It's a tantrum. And I don't appreciate it.' She opens the door for me to leave. 'It's important that you talk to Doctor Palmer in future. Not me.'

She walks into the waiting room, smiles at Miss Anorexic and asks her to wait in the office.

'I must go, Sophie,' she says, turning. 'And I'd like you to go, too.'

Then she walks away. Just like that.

The secretary has her smarmy face glued on my every move. I want to hit her. Hit everyone. Most of all myself. Choked with tears, I run to the exit door.

Outside in a small courtyard, I lie down on the path and sob. Helen doesn't want me. She never wanted me. My whole life is a charade. No one cares! I don't matter! It's not a tantrum! It's not! I love you! Helen, Helen, Helen – over and over – Helen, Helen.

People stop and stare. Others touch my arm – 'Are you all right?' I ignore them. Curled up, I lie there. Waiting. Helen is sure to come out. She'll see me from her window. She'll sit beside me, stroking my cheek, brushing away the tears.

'Come on, darlin'. Move yourself.'

Two security guards, one on each side of me.

'I'm not going! You can't make me! Get your hands off me!'

'C'mon, love. It's time to go. Up you get, on your feet. That's the way.'

I look up at Helen's window. She must be watching this. I won't be humiliated in front of her.

'All right!' I wrench my arms free of the guards. 'I'm going.'

My head held high I go with them, drained of all emotion except one. Love. For Helen. Something happened today that I can't explain. But if you truly love someone, you don't give up. You don't give up on love. Never, ever.

I still have Helen's poem in my pocket. Somehow I will get it to her.

23

*T*wo days go by. I hardly speak to Matt. He keeps asking what's wrong but I wouldn't know where to begin. He brings me hot drinks and makes me dinner – which I don't eat – and offers to take me to a doctor. And he gets little thanks for it. I try to sleep but dreams wait just below the surface, dreams with blood and screams. I wake in a sweat, too frightened to close my eyes again. Thoughts of cutting myself are ever-present. I would do it but I'm so exhausted.

'Sophie! I'm home!'

It's Amy.

'Can I come in?'

Oh no, no. I don't want to see anyone. I just want to . . .

'Coming in, ready or not.'

'No! Wait, Amy. It's great you're back – but please go and talk to Matt for a minute. I desperately need to take a shower. I'm still half asleep from medication. Okay?'

'Sure. Not a problem. Don't be long.'

I run the water cold, letting it shock me into some

kind of life. Soap. Shampoo. Toothpaste. Clean clothes and perfume. I'm ready.

'Amy.'

'Sophie!'

We embrace like long-lost sisters.

'Hey,' says Matt, 'don't I get any of the action?'

'Oh, all right.' Amy drags him into the huddle with us.

'How come you're home?' I ask. 'We just got a postcard saying you weren't coming back till next week.'

'Me and Johnny had a fight. I sure can pick 'em.' She rolls her eyes. 'Still, I had a terrific time after he took off. Met some cool guys. One in particular! I'll tell you every single detail – sit down, sit down.'

'Sorry to interrupt, gang.'

Matt holds his hand up like a schoolboy asking to be excused.

'Almost forgot to tell you, Sophie. You're supposed to be minding Joanne's kids,' he checks his watch, 'right about now.'

I fall down on the couch, groaning.

'Any other time I'd gladly do it,' I say, 'but I'm not up to it today.'

Matt offers no sympathy. 'Tough. You said you'd do it. Joanne's depending on you. You have to get over there.'

'Okay, okay, you're right.' I face Amy. 'Sorry. We'll catch up later.'

'It's not a problem.' She shrugs. 'I don't mind kids. You want me to help you?'

'Would you?'

'Yeah. Why not? I'll knee-cap them if they don't behave.'

I throw myself into her arms.

'Thank you, Ames.'

Knee-capping seems like a good idea within half an hour of being left alone with the boys. They're so wild; someone must have spiked their orange juice. However, Amy is in her element. She chases and tickles them until the house is wall-to-wall giggles.

Olivia sits quietly while I plait her hair. It is brown and lustrous and I feel proud of her, as if she's my daughter. If I had a daughter of my own I would never turn her away. There would be love waiting for her any time, day or night.

'Don't be sad.' Olivia's big eyes watch me curiously as I cry.

'I'm not sad, honey,' I lie. 'Just tired.'

The children are all tucked away in bed by nine and Amy and I flake out on the lounge.

'Give me all the goss,' she says. 'What's been happening while I was gone?'

I tell her about Marie's visit.

'Someone should put that cow down,' she snorts.

'But I think I'm safe for a while,' I assure her.

'Better be. I'll have a piece of that Marie if she tries to move you – sour-faced old dragon.'

Amy munches on almonds and washes them down with juice as she tells me about the infamous Johnny and his escapades. Then I hear about her daring travels on the back of Mick's motorbike – 'Mick is so hot, Soph – wait till you see him. And heaps nicer than bloody Johnny! I just love a guy on a Harley – I can't seem to help myself!'

All the while she talks I slip in and out: in the present with Amy, far away with Helen. For a while Amy's too caught up in her own story to notice, but when she does, she comes on strong.

'Hey. You haven't seen me in weeks. The least you can do is listen.'

I cover my eyes with both hands and bow my head, too tired to fight back or explain.

'What is it?' Her voice is softer now. 'What's up with you?'

'Nothing. Nothing.'

'Oh sure. Matt told me you've been upset about something. Look at me, Sophie – talk to me.'

I do look at her. Angrily. Tears course down my face. 'There's nothing wrong! Just leave me alone!'

For the next ten minutes we revert to being five years old. I guess sulking is like riding a bike, you never forget how to do it. Luckily, another thing you don't forget is how to make up.

Amy smiles. 'Hey, Soph? We friends?' she asks tentatively.

'You bet.' I put both my hands around hers.

Joanne comes in about midnight, meets Amy for the first time, and thanks us both profusely. Ten minutes later Amy and I are back at home. We say our goodnights and I flop into my bed and hug myself tightly.

It's been so hard tonight, Helen – missed you so much.

A few minutes later there's a tap on my door.

'Sophie. Can I come in?'

Why won't she leave me alone?

'I'm really tired, Ames. Can it wait until the morning?'

'No. Please let me in.'

'It's not locked,' I say.

Amy closes the door quietly behind her and sits at the foot of my bed. She's in her PJs, still wearing a wealth of silver bangles and rings.

'Now listen here, you.'

'Stop right there, Amy. I don't want a lecture.'

'Too bad. I'm not leaving this room until you tell me exactly what is going on.'

'I can't.'

'Is it Matt? Did he try something with you?'

'No. It's nothing like that.'

'Good. 'Cause I would've had to kill him. So what is it?'

'It's late – that's what it is.'

'Forget late. We're going to stay up all night until I get a truthful answer from you.'

179

'It's none of your business.' I start to cry. 'Please go away.'

'No chance. You've just got out of hospital and now you're falling apart again. Talk to me. I might be able to help. Just saying it might help. I'm your friend. Trust me!'

'All right!'

'Good.'

'If you tell this to anyone else . . .'

'It stays with me, Sophie. I promise.'

'This is so hard.'

'You can say anything to me.' She clutches my hand tightly. 'You can't shock me – I've done it all, Soph. Just say it.'

'. . . I love someone.'

'What?'

'You heard. Don't make me say it again.'

'In love? Well, that's a surprise.'

'It's really screwing me around.'

'It has to be Matt.'

'No. It isn't.'

'Oh god – he's gunna be so . . . You know he likes you, right?'

'Yes, Amy, I know that. But I can't help how I feel.'

'Of course you can't.'

'Please don't say anything to him.'

'Don't worry about that for a second. I won't say a word to anyone.'

'Thanks.'

'I don't know what to tell you, Soph. If you're in love you should be happy, but you're not happy. You're a wreck.'

'Oh, Amy.' The tears just cannot be stopped now. She's way off the mark thinking this is about some boy, but the anguish is there and I just can't explain it to her. To anyone.

'He doesn't love you? Is that what it is?'

'I don't know,' I splutter. 'I don't know. Please don't make me talk about it.'

'Come here.' Amy wraps her arms around me. 'You got boy troubles. That's normal. Boys are nothing but trouble. I thought I loved Johnny, too. But I got over it real quick. You just cry it all out, girl. I won't ask any more questions – but I'm here anytime you feel like talking. Don't worry, Soph. Everything's going to be fine.'

24

I don't know how long I lie on my bed, curled up with a physical pain that only eases when I touch Helen's photo. Such kindness in those eyes. I have to trust what I feel in my heart. You can't love someone without letting them know, without giving them a chance to return your love.

I leave home when it's still dark. The morning chill gnaws at my ears and fingers as I walk to the railway station. A train quickly arrives and I find a seat in a crowded carriage. I stare out the window, as so many others do. None of them see Helen's face. Only me. I hear her voice in every creak – *Sophie, Sophie* – wheels scraping on metal call me – *Sophie, Sophie* – and when the train sways, Helen rocks me, tenderly.

But then we go through a tunnel and I'm alone again in the darkness. She has such a grip on me. Without her I'm in a perpetual tunnel, even on the sunniest day. I don't think I want to live if I can't be with her.

Out of the train and my thumb is up as soon as I meet the road, begging for a ride. I stare into every car, my eyes pleading.

A station wagon pulls over to the gravel and I run to the driver's window. 'Can I get a lift? I really need to get home. My mum's been sick.'

He looks straight at my chest and then averts his eyes and smiles innocently when I catch him. Right now, I don't care.

'Yeah.' He shrugs. 'All right then.' He throws a bag into the back to make room for me in front. 'Hop in.'

I feel like I have to rehearse what I'm going to say to Helen, go over my lines like an actor. I wish it wasn't like that. If only we could be natural and spontaneous around each other. If only I could be sure of what to expect when she opens the door . . .

'You hitch rides very often?' The driver's gruff voice spears me back to reality. He has one hand on the steering wheel, the other rests on the seat close to my leg, palm up and fingers extended as if he's inviting me to move closer.

I shake my head without looking at him.

Edging further away, I retreat into my private world. It's a world of harmony and warmth. Helen is beside me; a mother protecting her child. I can feel her strong arms holding me. *You make me so happy*.

'What was that?' The driver stares across at me.

'I didn't say anything.'

A wry grin forms on his face. *Mad bitch*, he's thinking. Shortly afterwards, with both hands on the steering wheel, having ditched any hopes he might have had, he pulls over to the side of the road and stops the car.

'I'm turnin' off at the next set of lights. You better get out here.'

'Thanks,' I say, grateful to escape. 'That's fine.'

I step out of the car and take my bearings. How far to go? Three kays? Five? It could be a thousand and it wouldn't be too far. I'm heading towards Helen and I feel at peace.

There are fewer houses now. Only occasionally a car passes. I turn into her road and soon I'm walking along the driveway, my legs rubbery. Her car is parked in the carport. She's home.

No turning back now, Sophie.

I mount the stairs onto the veranda, and knock on the door. In the kitchen a radio is playing. I knock again, louder. The door flings open and Helen's standing there.

I smile and feel myself blushing. I want to throw my arms around her but all I can manage is, 'Hello.'

Helen steps out of her house and shuts the door behind her. 'What are you doing here?' Her words snap at me.

'I miss you.' My chin quivers. I start to cry. 'I think of you all the time, Helen. I just had to see you. Please understand. Please tell me it's all right.'

'How did you get here? How did you find out where I live?'

Snap. Snap.

'Who is it, Mum?'

Cara comes to the door.

'Go back inside, darling. It's just someone I know from the hospital. I won't be long.'

'Hi.' Cara smiles at me. 'Why are you crying?'

'Off you go,' Helen says firmly. 'Now, please.'

As she closes the door on Cara, she turns on me.

'You shouldn't be here, Sophie. This is my home. There are boundaries. I see patients at my office. Not at my home.'

I feel so small, so empty.

'Do you understand me? Do you?'

'I tried to see you at the hospital.'

'And I told you that your therapist is Doctor Palmer. Do you recall me saying that? I said it very plainly.'

'I don't want him, Helen. All I want is you.'

'You're testing my patience, Sophie.' She pushes a handkerchief at me. 'How did you get here?'

Sniffling, sobbing, I mutter, 'I hitched a ride from the station.'

'And how did you find out my address?'

'I don't know – I'm sorry, I'm sorry.'

She sighs heavily. 'Honestly, Sophie, this is too much. Wait here.'

I crouch down and rock back and forth, a moan pouring out of me in one long river of pain. Then Helen is back, clutching her car keys.

'I'm taking you to the station. Pick yourself up.'

'But Helen –'

'We're going now.'

No sooner have I buckled up than the car speeds away.

'Please don't be angry with me, Helen. I just wanted to see you. I'd never, ever do anything to hurt you.'

'I *am* angry. You must have known that coming to my house would upset me and my daughter. It's a terrible thing to do.'

Her every word slashes me, though not like a razor's cut. These words gouge deep into me and will never, never heal.

'Please forgive me.' I cover my pathetic face. 'I didn't know it was bad.'

I peer through my fingers and see her staring ahead, without a glimmer of compassion.

'I'm disappointed in you, Sophie. Very disappointed.'

The station looms ahead.

'I'll talk to Doctor Palmer about this and he'll be in touch with you. From now on, you deal with him. Tell me that you understand that.'

'I understand.'

'Good. Now I want you to go straight home.' Helen stops the car and looks pointedly at my door. I open it and step out. 'Can I trust you to do that? To go straight home?'

I nod like a small, naughty child who's being sent to stand in a corner.

'Sophie. Listen very closely. If you ever do this again, I'll be forced to call the police to remove you.' The words wash over me. I'm numb. 'I don't want to do that, but I will. You hear me, Sophie? I will call the police.'

Then she is away, driving back to her home and I am left, feeling more alone in the world than I ever thought possible.

I ride the train. I cry.

I walk. I cry.

Helen's words play over and over in my head.

'*Disappointed.*'

'*Call the police.*'

'*Do you understand?*'

'*Do you? Do you?*'

At home Matt and Amy are eating in front of the television.

'Hi, Sophie!' Amy calls. Matt looks up and smiles. I rush into the bathroom. In seconds I'm naked under the shower, the water raining down on me. There's a razor in my hand.

I slash myself, once, twice.

My arm bright red with blood.

Three times.

Bloody water pools at my feet.

Four times, five. My chest and stomach.

I howl with the pain, the relief.

And then I'm on the floor of the shower sobbing one word again and again.

Helen.

Amy's hammering on the door. 'Sophie! What's wrong? What's the matter?'

The door flings open and Amy's standing there, staring at me, her mouth gaping. 'Christ, Sophie, what the hell are you doing?'

I beg her to go away. And then there's nothing but darkness.

25

*A*my throws opens the blinds and sunlight streams in. It's a whole new day. Kids ride past on bikes. Their laughter floats up to me and I feel such a pang of sadness for things lost.

'Good morning, Sleeping Beauty.' Amy plops herself on the bed. 'Feel like some brekkie? Matt's cooking.'

The cuts from yesterday sting, but worse is the guilt I feel, the humiliation.

'What time is it?'

'Ten. How you doing?'

'I feel hung over. Got a huge headache.'

'Yeah, the doctor said that might happen.'

'What doctor?'

'You don't remember?'

'No.'

'You really scared me, Soph. I had to call a GP. He gave you a needle to calm you down. He said the cuts weren't too deep so I just put some cream on them.'

The air reeks with the smell of ointment. It's stained the sheets around my chest a dirty yellow colour that almost matches my nightdress, tinged with blood from the slashing.

'Amy, I'm sorry.'

'No dramas. Just as well Matt was here, though.'

'Matt? He saw?'

'Of course he did. He helped me get you out of the shower.'

'Oh, shit.'

'Hey, Soph, you had blood everywhere and I was freaked. As far as I knew, you were bleeding to death. I had to get Matt to help.'

'I never want to see him again,' I mutter. 'Never.'

'Matt doesn't think any less of you, you goose. He's not like that. Haven't you worked him out yet?'

The knowledge that Matt and Amy care for me brings on a fresh stream of tears. I wasn't really sure before but now I am.

'I'm here. It's okay.' Amy strokes my hair, on and on.

'I just want to hide,' I say. 'For the rest of my life.'

'Pity about that.' Amy pulls the blankets on the floor, then the sheet. 'You're getting up and having something to eat. No arguments.'

I struggle out of bed, cursing her under my breath.

'Hey, Matt,' Amy calls into the kitchen. 'Sophie's awake. And she's starving!'

I shudder.

After I've showered – quickly, painfully – I dress

and go out to face the world, or at least my small corner of it. It's pure hell walking into the kitchen, seeing Matt after the way he's seen me. He relieves my agony with a smile. I'm sure it's given out of pity, but then I feel the rough bristles of his unshaved face brush against me as he unexpectedly pecks me on the cheek. And then he hugs me. It's only for a few seconds but it feels incredibly good.

Amy and I sit at the table and Matt carries in our plates.

'I'm so sorry about . . .' That's as far as I get.

'Ancient history,' he breaks in. 'I'm giving you two eggs. That okay?'

I feel better with each bite. There are no lectures or questions. They both saw me with my body slashed by my own hands, and they still accept me. But then I notice Amy giving Matt a look, prompting him to say something.

'Sophie.'

Hesitantly he places a hand on top of mine. I sense trouble.

'What is it? Did I do something bad that I've forgotten? I didn't hurt anyone, did I?'

Amy answers. 'No, no. It's nothing like that. We looked in your address book when you were out of it, that's all.'

'To get the number of your doctor,' Matt adds.

They rang Helen?

'We thought we should ring him.'

'*Him*? You mean Noel?'

'Yeah. It seemed the right thing to do, since he's been treating you. You don't mind, do you?'

'He doesn't matter,' I say, incredibly relieved.

'Bloody doctors.' Amy shakes her head. 'He wanted to put you back in hospital, but Matt talked him out of it.'

Matt grins. 'I told him to butt out.'

'You didn't say that, did you?'

'Well, not exactly those words but I got the message across. I couldn't let you go, Soph. You're the only one around here who likes my cooking.'

But then Amy gets to the sharp end of the story.

'This Noel guy, he insisted on seeing you today.'

'Sorry,' Matt adds, 'couldn't talk him out of it. I'll drive you there.'

'No thanks. I'm okay to go by myself. I'm a big girl.'

'You should really let him take you,' Amy says. 'You can't be a hundred per cent after what you've just been through.'

Anger flares inside me. I hate it when other people try to take control of my life. They always do it to 'help' me as if I'm incapable of making my own decisions. And now Matt and Amy have joined the club, ringing Noel, making an appointment for me, talking about me behind my back.

Now it's Matt's turn again.

'I won't come into his office with you. I'll just drive – that's it. Will you let me do that much for you, Sophie?'

'No. I won't. I'm going to bed.' I push back my chair and stand. 'I'm sick of talking. I don't want to talk to anyone – especially not Noel.'

Amy blocks my path, hands on her hips. 'You owe us, Sophie.'

'What are you talking about? I don't owe you anything. Get out of my way.'

'Yes, you do owe us. We took turns staying with you every minute while you were off your head. Now you can pay us back by getting better. Go with Matt. See the bloody doctor.'

'Fine! I will! But I'm going on my own. I don't need Matt to hold my hand. I'm not a child!'

'Then stop acting like one.' Amy says it quietly but it hits me hard. She aims a final glare in my direction before marching from the room.

Matt bites into a slice of toast, making sure not to look at me.

'You're probably as fed up with me as she is,' I say. 'You'd have to be.'

'No, I'm not.'

'Come on, Matt. Amy was honest, why don't you try it? Tell me how you really feel about what I did. Go on, don't let it fester. Just get it over with and tell me.'

'That's easy, Sophie. Repulsed. Sickened. Revolted. When I saw you in that shower I experienced all of those things.'

A wave of nausea washes over me.

'But I didn't feel that way because of how you looked.' Matt comes over and touches my face. 'It was because I knew how sad you must have been to do that to yourself. No one should be that sad.'

I can write poems for Helen; build them out of air and empty dreams. But the right words to say to Matt scurry away when I search for them. All I can do is lean my head against his chest and let him hold me.

Noel's voice drones on, filling his office.

'You've been cutting yourself for a long time, haven't you?'

I'm sitting in my usual chair, eyes closed. Matt is waiting in the car for me. He and Amy, they are true friends . . . but I can't compare them with Helen. I know it's not the right thing to do, but I still love her.

'Self harm is not unusual, Sophie.'

I look up at him.

'People in emotional pain often cut themselves. Some say that the physical pain relieves their intense, sometimes overwhelming, feelings.'

My tears flow again and he pauses as I pull a tissue from the box.

'It's only natural that you'd feel distressed at Doctor Marshall turning you away.'

That stuns me. I've been so careful not to let Noel into my life, and now he knows everything.

'I got a call from her. She told me what happened.'

'She said she'd call the police.'

'You must be feeling very angry with her.' Noel's voice is so soft I strain to hear what he's saying.

'No, no. I'm not angry.'

'Would you like to tell me how you are feeling?'

I stare at the floor, shutting him out, but eventually his words intrude.

'Do you know why she would want to call the police?'

'There was no reason in the world for her to say that. She knows me better than anyone. I would never hurt her. Never!' I jump out of my chair and stride to the door. Noel walks over casually to see me out, as unruffled as ever.

'Are you quite sure you want to leave? I don't mind at all if you don't feel like talking. We can just sit here. It's your time.'

'No! Not today. I have to go. Please let me go.'

'You'll be all right? You won't harm yourself?'

I shake my head. 'Matt's waiting for me in the car.'

'Good. That's good. I spoke to him on the phone. He seems like a very nice young man.'

He doesn't get as much as a sideways glance from me as I brush past him.

Matt opens the car door and his smile – so full of hope – breaks me in two. In tears, I say, 'I'm sorry, Matt. I'm so sorry.'

Days pass. I live on my own island, all but cut off from Matt and Amy. We talk briefly and sometimes eat meals together but my heart is always with Helen. Swirling above all else is the memory of her sending me away. I see the anger and coldness in her eyes, hear it in her voice. The image won't go away. I feel so wounded, yet the thought of forgetting her is too painful to consider. Instead, I spend every moment thinking of how I can turn it around. How can I stop Helen from being angry with me? How can I find my way back into her arms?

Matt is Mr Patient. He understands that I need space and he gives it to me: perhaps he needs space from me, too. Greta comes to visit but I tell her I'm sick and send her away. I send everyone away, including Amy. She jumps at the chance when Mick, the new boyfriend with the Harley – suggests a holiday with him.

'You don't mind, do you, Sophie? I'll be back in two weeks.'

'Of course I don't mind,' I say, blank-faced. 'Have a great time.'

It's just me and Matt then. He hasn't given up on

me. One night he suggests we go to the movies and I haven't got the heart to turn him down. This is a movie hand-picked to make me feel happy; lots of laughs, dancing and singing. I really do try to enjoy it but everything is too loud and shrill. I close my eyes and block my ears. We're out of there after twenty minutes. Matt doesn't say anything on the way home; he just holds my hand.

In the morning I resolve to keep busy. Helen told me that once. I remember everything she ever said.

If you're feeling depressed, you have to fight it. Get on your feet. Work up a sweat. Physical activity alters brain chemistry and can promote feelings of wellbeing.

I vacuum the carpets and clean the floors – *Helen, Helen* – I sit at the kitchen table with a pile of school-work in front of me, determined to make a dent in it – *Helen, Helen*.

There is nothing I can do to keep her away. So I go to her again. This time in words.

Dearest Helen,

I came to you in peace. As a friend. I can't understand why you said you would call the police. I can't get you out of my mind. It's impossible to forget you. Please don't be angry with me. And please please please let me come and see you again. This time in your office. Would you please make an appointment for me? I desperately need to see you, to talk to you, even if it's only to learn how to live without you. Sophie x

As I write that last line, tears run down my cheeks

and plop onto the page. I walk to the corner letterbox and post it.

'She'll write back,' I tell myself. 'I know she will.'

I spend the next few days anxiously waiting to hear from Helen. Every time the phone rings I dive for it. She doesn't call. I wait by the letterbox for the daily delivery. Nothing. The new term has resumed: I'm supposed to have returned to school. I contemplate not ever going back; I can't face anyone there. In my sessions with Noel I weep continually, telling him how sad I am at not hearing from Helen.

'Sophie,' he says in his ever-neutral tone, 'you may have to accept that Doctor Marshall doesn't want to be in touch with you.'

'No! I don't believe that. You're wrong!'

Again Noel opens the door for me to escape back into the real world, except for me there is no escape.

I spend hours writing about Helen in my journal, and then a poem begins to form . . .

Inside me you crouch
Like a bruised shadow
Forever haunting;
You whisper my name at night,
Through the endless hours,
Daily I feel your rhythms,
Smell your skin,
The imprint of your body.
Every moment

I attempt to tiptoe
Away from you,
Yet here you are,
Galloping across my mind
With footsteps
Heavy as my aching need of you.

26

The postman arrives on the fifth day. No word from Helen. I can't stand it any longer. I simply have to see her.

Today she will be at her city practice. She talked about it once. I feel more confident about seeing her there. She works with three other psychiatrists so she won't be as busy as she is at the hospital. She'll have time to talk to me. We'll sit in her office and I'll give her my new poem. This is my final chance. I know I'm risking everything, but I tell myself that when she reads it, she'll know how desperate my need is to be with her. Once she really understands, she won't turn me away.

Matt is ironing his clothes when I announce I'm going out.

'Where are you off to?'

Lately he's become so protective, it's like he's my guardian – my unwanted bodyguard.

'Nowhere.'

He switches off the iron. 'You shouldn't be on your own when you're like this.'

'Like what?'

'You know what I'm talking about, Soph. Let me come with you.'

'No!'

'Sophie!'

'Get out of my way!'

He grabs me by the wrists.

'Let's just bloody talk about this! You're acting stupid!'

'You bastard!'

I kick him in the shin, as hard as I can.

'Christ!'

The second he drops his hands I storm out of the house, slamming the door behind me. It opens again and Matt is yelling. 'Come back here! Now!'

'Go away!' I shout. He slows to pull on a coat but keeps coming. I run down the street and, turning back, I see him running, too. Breathless, I reach the train station. I'm scrabbling through my pocket for coins to buy a ticket when Matt touches my arm. 'Soph. I'm tired of chasing you. Come back home.'

I pretend he's not there and walk away from him. He doesn't try to talk to me but when I catch the next train, he gets on it, too. Seething, I watch as he moves from seat to seat, until he's sitting across the aisle from me.

'For the last time, Matt, stop following me!' Other passengers turn and stare. He fiddles with his shirt sleeve.

'Didn't you hear me? I said, LEAVE ME ALONE!'

'Sophie, I'm your friend . . .'

'I'll jump off the train. Is that what you want? I'll jump off the train!'

'Okay, I'll go. Calm down. I'll go.' He moves away into the adjoining carriage. And I stare down every prying eye that glances at me.

At Helen's station I'm the first out of the train, the only passenger who runs up the steps. Through the ticket barrier, I'm out onto the street – and there's no sign of Matt.

Helen's waiting room.

'I need to see Helen,' I tell the secretary. 'Doctor Marshall.'

'Do you have an appointment?'

I shake my head. 'It's urgent.'

'She won't be able to see you.' The bitch doesn't even consider it.

'Thanks a lot!' I snap at her. 'You could at least have tried to help!'

'Sophie.' Suddenly Helen's at my elbow.

I smile at her. Hopefully. Pleadingly.

'I need to see you. Did you get my letter? Helen, I miss you so much.'

'Go into my office,' she says curtly.

I obey. I have the poem open in my hands, ready to thrust it at her: it's the only thing that can save me.

Helen appears a short time later and sits at her desk, staring at me unrelentingly.

Finally, 'Sophie, I am becoming very, very annoyed.'

'I've got this poem for you . . .'

'Be quiet, please. I want you to stop pursuing me. It's harassment. I do not want to ever see you – anywhere. Not at my work. Nor at the hospital. Nowhere near my home. I don't want to see you, period. Should I write it down? Should I make a list for you? I don't want there to be any misunderstanding.'

I feel heat rise up my neck and into my face. *She doesn't want me. She doesn't want me.* The sentence swells in my head till it feels like my brain is going to burst.

'You can't treat me like this!' I yell. 'You hugged me! You loved me! You! You! You!'

My eyes blur with tears and I storm out of there, swiping a hand across her desk as I go, sending pens and papers flying. All I'm aware of is Helen's rejecting eyes, carved into my mind forever like the slash marks of a razor.

I feel as though I've been in a train crash and need to escape. Can't breathe. Need to get into the open air, as far away as possible. Out on the street I push past people but I don't know where I'm going. There is nowhere to go.

'Sophie. Wait.'

Matt stands in the middle of the street, a stream of cars stopping him from crossing over. I run away from him again and find myself in the front garden of a block of units, hiding behind an overgrown shrub. My breathing is scrambled and so are my thoughts. I know there's someone after me, but it isn't Matt, it's some kind of monster. I feel him tearing at my skin and dash out, looking for someone to help me. But there he is, racing up to me, reaching out, grabbing my arm. I scream and scream. A passer-by rushes to my aid. 'Call the police!' I beg her. 'He keeps stalking me!' I run without looking back.

Some time later – minutes, hours – I find myself inside a complex of offices. A security guard is questioning me. I have no idea where I am, hardly any idea of who I am, or how I came to be here. Then I hear myself swearing at the man. I flee from him, and only stop running when I jump into an unoccupied elevator. All I can think of is Helen, pale and slack-jawed as I rushed past. Her words pound in my head – *I do not want to ever see you – anywhere. I don't want to see you, period.*

I walk into a mall and take a seat in a coffee shop. I need to find Helen. I need to give her my poem.

A man comes over to take my order. Only then do I realise that I left home without my wallet.

'Sorry.' I stand up to leave. 'I don't have any money.'

I must look such a sight, my face beaten up by tears, my clothes dirty from some fall I can't remember. Most people would be glad to see the back of me, but this man is different.

'Stay there,' he says gently. 'I'll get you a coffee and a sandwich. You look like you need it.'

'But I can't pay you.'

He smiles. 'You don't have to.'

I cry then for his kindness, for my confused and aching self.

And then there is Matt. He finds me late in the afternoon. I'm slumped in the gutter outside Helen's office. He crouches in front of me.

'How you doin', Soph?'

I lean into him and close my eyes. 'I've been so lost,' I mutter.

He helps me to my feet. 'I'll have you home soon.'

'But I came back here to give Helen my poem. I just got too tired but I'm all right again now.'

'Helen doesn't want to see you.'

'She does. She does.'

'No. You have to forget about her.'

'Matt, please.' I squeeze his hand tightly. 'I'll give her my poem and go. It'll just take a few minutes.'

'All right then. But only if I can come with you.'

There's no more fight left in me – but it's more than that.

'Yes,' I reply. 'I want you to be there.'

We sit in the waiting room, my arm laced around Matt's waist, my head on his shoulder. I fall into a deep sleep, for once not tormented by ugly visions.

Then Matt nudges me. I know Helen is there but I can't bear to look at her. I hang my head and see her black shoes standing near us, hear her saying, 'Please take Sophie home. You must convince her not to come to see me again.'

I hold out my poem.

'No, Sophie. I don't want it.'

And then she is gone.

27

*A*t home I fall asleep on the couch. Matt pushes two chairs together and uses them as a bed for his lanky frame. I have frightening dreams, as I always do, but now when I wake Matt is there with soft words and kindness. I lie there grieving for Helen's lost love but realising at the same time it's all so selfish, this need, this fathomless need. Somehow I have to claw my way out of the hole I'm in. Matt is the only constant in my upside-down world. I have to try for him.

In the morning when he says that he's driving me to my appointment with Noel – 'whether I like it or not'– I shock him by saying, 'I like it.'

'You do?'

'As long as you don't go any further than the waiting room.'

'Sounds like a good plan.'

Noel is surprised to see Matt waiting outside. He looks at me quizzically and when I don't respond, he asks directly, 'Is that the young man I've spoken to on the phone?'

'Yes. Matt,' I volunteer.

Noel gives me his usual bland smile.

'So what's been happening, Sophie?'

Sighing, I make myself go back into hell. Tell him all that I can remember of the day before. Noel listens, his face unreadable.

There's the predictable pause when I've finished – like a long agonising punctuation mark.

Then: 'What are your feelings today?'

'I can't believe that Helen doesn't want me. I've done nothing but love her. And she's tossed me aside like a piece of junk.' Tears burn the back of my lids.

'And how is it, Sophie, that you think Doctor Marshall should act?'

Perhaps, for the first time, I know the answer. I put my hands over my ears and keep them plugged. If I close my eyes I might be able to see Helen, feel her hug me once again. I try so hard but I can't. There's only blackness and that answer, pressing down on me. I know now she will never want me – but I still can't say it.

'Do you think that you might want to hurt yourself again, Sophie?' Noel's voice rolls out, buttery smooth.

'I don't know what I'm thinking.'

'You don't want to tell me?'

'Please. Noel. Leave me alone, will you? You're

always trying to dig into my brain.'

He stares back at me, his face expressionless.

'I've had enough!'

I bolt for the door. Noel doesn't try to stop me. He doesn't care. I charge into the waiting room, ignore Matt and continue out into the street.

At the next corner Matt catches up with me and grabs my arm. 'Just stop right there.'

'Let go of me!'

'Not this time. You have to stop this, Sophie.'

'I've got nothing to live for.' I'm bawling my eyes out.

He grips me tighter. 'That's not true.'

'You don't get it! Helen doesn't want me! There's nothing to live for!'

'You've got plenty to live for!'

'Yeah, name one thing!'

'What about me? I'm here. Don't I count for any-thing? Don't I matter?'

'I share a house with you, Matt – that's all!'

'But it could be more than that. I care about you, Sophie.'

'Then you're stupid,' I say. 'It's impossible – *I'm* impossible.'

'No, Sophie. The only thing's that's impossible is Helen. She's a dream. You have to learn to live in the real world.'

'She's real to me,' I sob. 'You don't understand. She's my mother. Please don't say she's not real.'

People pass us in the street, but I scarcely notice them. Matt draws me close.

I allow myself to fold into him and he holds me for the longest time.

'I'm real,' he tells me.

That night Matt says, 'I don't want you to be alone tonight, Soph. I want to sleep next to you. Make sure you feel safe. I'm not going to make any moves. I just want you to know I'm here for you.'

We lie in my bed face to face, our nose tips touching lightly. I look into his eyes which are green like the pool on a sunny day. He has a tiny mole just under his right eye and the hint of a scar on his cheek. It feels like I'm seeing him for the first time, discovering him.

We're quiet for a long time. There's no need for words. Finally, when I do speak, it's not what Matt wants to hear. I can't help it.

'I loved her,' is all I can say. 'I really loved her.'

Matt wipes away my tears and holds me, just holds me, all night long.

In the following days I feel life seeping back into my body. When I write in my journal it's about Matt. I think about how he hugged me after I'd run away from him all day. It is still warm in my mind and the words tumble out easily . . .

This is the most tender moment of all –

Your arms enclosing my brittle parcel
Of bones and organs and fear.
The comfort is exquisite.

Soon Amy arrives home, blazing with enough energy to light up a small town.

She's barely through the door before she takes off at a gallop, telling me and Matt all about Mick. 'He's a bit of a Goth. But not one of those really weird dudes. He's so cool. You've got to meet him!'

Later she sees Matt kissing me on the cheek. It's different from other times. She knows we're closer. Amy's usual style would be to make a very loud and immediate comment, but this time she manages to contain herself until Matt is out of earshot.

'You said there was someone else,' she reminds me. 'But now it seems like . . .'

'Things change,' I answer.

She hugs me. And I think to myself, *so this is what happiness feels like*.

My mind is clearer and I finally feel ready to face school. I arrive late to avoid having to confront inquisitive classmates. In the Science room, first period, I become aware that some people are studiously avoiding me while others smile briefly before pretending to be engrossed in their note-taking.

Then it's recess: kids milling in corridors exchanging greetings, gossiping, or rushing by, trying to beat the canteen crush, and me speeding out of the building to avoid everyone. I sit on a bench in the schoolyard, hunched over my diary, trying to see what class I have next, but all the time certain I have an audience. Teachers, lifting cups to their mouths, crowd around the staffroom window as though to point me out.

'Come and look at the freak,' I mutter.

'Hey, Soph!' Greta stands in front of me, feet apart, school bag between them. 'Finally you're back in the land of the living . . .'

She sets herself down beside me. 'So, tell me all about it. I want every single detail. All about the crazies.'

Her total disregard for anything resembling political correctness makes me laugh. She always has this effect on me. I love her for it.

'Is this mania?' She peers closely at me, adopting the pose, actions and facial features of a demented shrink. 'Ah, I see vee vill have to cut open zee bootiful cranium and examine zee brain! Vot bloody mess vee vill find, I vunder?'

She goes on and on, playing the mad professor and I'm enjoying every second of it. A couple of girls come over and join in the fun. We're all together being stupid and it feels so good, so normal.

I'm in Noel's office, checking out the new picture on his wall. In a bushland setting, a woman is swimming away from me, past deckchairs and umbrellas, towards a blue sky brushed with clouds.

'You like it?'

'Yes. Great photo.'

'It's my wife. I took it on our holiday.'

'You have a wife?'

He smiles slyly. And then I know he has deliberately revealed this information and is looking for my response.

A fuzzy image of Noel and his wife lying together spins briefly in, and then out, of my mind.

'I hope you're happy together,' I say, determined not to know more. I feel proud of myself for holding back. It's like at last I've learnt something – I'll never be part of Noel's life so I should just stay out of it. If only I'd been able to do that with Helen . . .

'What are you thinking of today, Sophie?' Noel is positioned in front of the beautiful kaleidoscope poster, his fingers in their usual church-steeple position.

I shrug. 'It's always Helen. She never leaves.' For the millionth time I feel my face break apart as the thought of her rips through me. 'Is it ever going to end, Noel?'

'In time, Sophie, yes, I think it will.' His usual impassive face changes. I see tenderness. 'I don't know how long it will take. No one does. But every day you come a little further.'

Time clicks past and I listen to the thud of each second. Noel sits there like some Buddha figure;

unfailingly calm and wise. I wish I knew the secret of how to be like that, but maybe it's only luck. I've got scars that run so deep and go back so long; the kind of hurts Noel has never known. But somehow I have to let them go. If I don't, I'm going to be sitting in a shrink's office all my sorry life, counting off the seconds.

'It's so indulgent, all this analysing,' I say at last. 'I could be out with Matt, having a good time.'

'That sounds very positive.'

He glances at the wall clock and I know the session has swung to its end.

Noel takes a tissue and sneezes. At the door I thank him for his time. And then I walk up the side path of his office to the front gate, where Matt is waiting for me. The day is young and shining.

ACKNOWLEDGEMENTS:

During the writing of this novel, a number of people gave me invaluable feedback, for which I thank them sincerely. They were Jenny Mounfield, Peta Fraser, Dr Virginia Lowe, Ann Whitehead, Sandy Fussell, Maureen Johnson, Sue Whiting, Vicki Stanton, my agent Debbie Golvan, and most especially, my author husband, Bill Condon. I also thank Andrew Leon and Julie Blaze for their compassion and care, and my publisher Paul Collins for investing his faith in this book, and editor Saralinda Turner for her astute and helpful advice.